S

If she continued to see Fox, sooner or later their mutual passion would burst out of control, but the thought of not seeing him any more was unbearable.

She'd never felt like this before, and her experience with men was so limited that she was unable to determine how to handle it. She couldn't become just another one of Fox's lovers, but she couldn't give him up, either. With him, she was alive in a way that was new to her. Up until the time she met him, her books and studies and quiet life had been sufficient.

She hadn't known what she was missing, like a person born blind who can't appreciate the glory of a sun he has never seen. But now she couldn't go back to that former existence.

It would never again be enough.

Dear Reader,

Welcome to Silhouette! Our goal is to give you hours of unbeatable reading pleasure, and we hope you'll enjoy each month's six new Silhouette Desires. These sensual, provocative love stories are both believable and compelling—sometimes they're poignant, sometimes humorous, but always enjoyable.

Indulge yourself. Experience all the passion and excitement of falling in love along with our heroine as she meets the irresistible man of her dreams and together they overcome all obstacles in the path to a happy ending.

If this is your first Desire, I hope it'll be the first of many. If you're already a Silhouette Desire reader, thanks for your support! Look for some of your favorite authors in the coming months: Stephanie James, Diana Palmer, Dixie Browning, Ann Major and Doreen Owens Malek, to name just a few.

Happy reading!

Isabel Swift
Senior Editor

SDRL-7/85

DOREEN OWENS MALEK
Desperado

Silhouette Desire
Published by Silhouette Books New York
America's Publisher of Contemporary Romance

SILHOUETTE BOOKS
300 E. 42nd St., New York, N.Y. 10017

ISBN: 0-373-05260-X

First Silhouette Books printing February 1986

America's Publisher of Contemporary Romance

Printed in the U.S.A.

Books by Doreen Owens Malek

Silhouette Romance

The Crystal Unicorn #363

Silhouette Special Edition

A Ruling Passion #154

Silhouette Desire

Native Season #86
Reckless Moon #222
Winter Meeting #240
Desperado #260

Silhouette Intimate Moments

The Eden Tree #88
Devil's Deception #105

DOREEN OWENS MALEK

is an attorney and former teacher who decided on her current career when she sold her fledgling novel to the first editor who read it. She has been writing ever since. Born and raised in New Jersey, she has lived throughout the northeast and now makes her home in Pennsylvania.

For my godchildren,
Keith Frances Malek and Stephen Baldwin Freiberger

One

The Florida sun was losing strength, but still brilliant, as Cindy and Paula emerged from the restaurant in late afternoon. Cindy shielded her eyes, and then dropped her hand when they turned to walk down the street.

"How far is it to your apartment?" Cindy asked, watching as her friend pulled a pair of sunglasses from her purse and put them on.

"A couple of miles," Paula replied. "The complex is right outside of town."

Cindy nodded. Paula had picked her up at the Clearwater airport a couple of hours before, and they had stopped for a bite in Council Rock before traveling on to Paula's house.

"When are you going to start the research?" Paula asked, rummaging in her shoulder bag for her car keys.

"Monday, I guess." Cindy smiled slightly. They'd spent the whole meal catching up on their social lives and had never discussed in detail the reason for Cindy's visit.

"So you've already contacted somebody from the university," Paula said.

"Yes, the department chairman is going to see me." Cindy was a graduate assistant in the folklore department of the University of Pennsylvania. The subject of her master's thesis was the legends of the Seminole Indians, and she'd come to northern Florida to research the topic in the section of the country where the Seminoles had lived for hundreds of years. Paula was a college friend who'd offered to have Cindy stay with her when she heard that Cindy's work was taking her to the Tampa area.

"What about your supervisor?" Paula inquired, glancing at Cindy.

"I have to mail him my ideas and get approval of my outline, but I don't think that will be difficult. He's working in the field himself."

"Huh," Paula replied skeptically, snaring her keys and then holding them aloft like a trophy. "Good luck to him. That egghead stuff you write all looks like nonsense to me."

Cindy was about to reply when a thunderous crash made both women spin around and then jump back. In disbelief, Cindy watched as the picture window of a hardware store fronting the street exploded into sparkling smithereens. Glass fragments flew in all directions as two figures hurtled through the window. Cindy and Paula both threw up their arms to cover their faces. Shards tinkled to the ground as the men who'd shattered the window tumbled to the walkway, almost at Cindy's feet, rolling over and over, locked in combat.

When the glass finally stopped falling, Cindy peeked through her fingers to see what was happening. One of the men was flat on the ground, face down, with his arms pinned behind him. The other was sitting astride him snapping handcuffs on his wrists.

Cindy looked at Paula, who appeared remarkably undisturbed by the whole episode, observing calmly as the taller man hauled the captive to his feet. Cindy turned her head to watch also. The prisoner stumbled along unwillingly as the victor dragged him to a pickup truck parked at the curb and unceremoniously cuffed him to the rear bumper.

Cindy leaned in to her companion and said in an undertone, "Paula, what is going *on* here?"

Paula shrugged. "It's just Drew Fox bringing in another one."

"Another *what*?" Cindy demanded, bewildered.

Before Paula could reply, the front door of the store flew open, and an irate man, obviously the owner, started berating the tall man in a loud voice, to the vast entertainment of the small crowd that had gathered. The object of his tirade patted his shoulder reassuringly, speaking to him in a low, comforting tone. Mollified, the proprietor calmed down, and was even managing a small smile when a patrol car glided silently to a stop in the street, its blue light pulsating. The fettered prisoner looked on grimly, resigned to his fate.

"Cheese it, the cops," Paula muttered, and Cindy grinned. There was something amusing about this scene, which shouldn't have been funny. But the non-chalant stance of the man who had initiated it all, lounging with his hands in his pockets and greeting the policemen affably as if he were the host at a block party, struck her as absurd.

"Look at that guy," she said to Paula. "You'd never think he just splintered a pane of glass with his head."

Paula chuckled in response, and the two women watched as the police took charge of the prisoner and led him away to the patrol car. As soon as it pulled away, the crowd began to disperse and the tall man sauntered over to them, pushing his hair back from his forehead.

"Hi, short stuff," he said casually, talking to Paula, but looking at Cindy.

"You're out of date, Fox," Paula replied dryly. "My brother stopped calling me that when I was twelve."

"You still look pretty short to me," Fox observed, smiling just a little, with his eyes, which remained on Cindy's face.

"Everybody looks short to you," Paula said.

"Are you ladies all right?" he asked. "Some of that glass came pretty close to you."

"We're fine," Paula replied, for both of them. "But I can't say the same for you. You do realize that you're bleeding?"

Fox blinked, surprised, and put his hand to his head again. It came away stained red.

"I thought my hair felt wet," he said. He pulled a handkerchief from the back pocket of his jeans and tied it around his head like a bandanna.

"Oh, very good," Paula said. "Nice and sanitary. Why don't you come by the emergency room tonight and I'll tape that up for you."

Paula was a nurse who worked the night shift at Lykes Hospital. "I just might do that," Fox replied, still watching Cindy.

"I'm surprised to see you jumping through windows again, Drew," Paula said. "It reminds me of the old days. I thought you'd long ago graduated to international criminal types."

"I was doing a favor for Sheriff Tully," Fox replied. "That joker escaped from his jail. I chased him into Barney's store from the alley out back." He glanced at Paula, then his gaze returned to Cindy. "Who's your friend?"

"I've missed you too, Fox," Paula observed acidly, and he grinned.

"Andrew Fox," he said to Cindy, extending his hand. Cindy grasped it.

"Lucinda Warren," she replied, her fingers lost in his big palm.

"Lucinda," he repeated. "Sounds like the princess in a fairy tale."

"Everybody calls me Cindy," she responded softly, mesmerized by his green eyes, which swept over her face, taking in every detail.

"But I'm not everybody, Lucinda," he replied, continuing to hold her hand. He towered over her, his big, compact body at ease, and yet somehow alert, as if he were ready for anything at any moment.

He's Indian, Cindy thought, gazing up at him in mute absorption. She could see it in his straight, midnight hair and in the dusky skin, a combination of copper and terra cotta, which complemented his high cheekbones and strong, prominent nose. His other features were European, however: light eyes and a finely molded, thin-lipped mouth. It was an arresting combination, a harmony of opposites that made him, not handsome, but unforgettable.

"What are you doing in town?" he asked, his tone muted, intimate.

"I'm researching my master's thesis at Gulf Coast University. I'll be staying with Paula for several weeks."

He accepted this without comment and then released her hand slowly. As he let go, his two middle finger curled around hers possessively, and then fell away. He turned to Paula, as if remembering suddenly that she was present.

"Say hello to Johnny for me when you see him," he directed. "I'll try to stop by the hospital tonight for some T.L.C." He smiled wickedly.

"Don't forget," Paula advised him. "That gash looks pretty bad; you shouldn't neglect it."

"I'll live," he said lightly. He looked at Cindy again and said, with a slight inclination of his dark head, "Welcome to Florida, ma'am." Then he loped back to his truck and swung up into the cab, slamming the door shut behind him in one economical movement. Both women remained looking after him until the truck roared away into the distance.

"Kind of unsettling, isn't he?" Paula commented, with a sly, sideward glance.

"What was all that about?" Cindy countered, ignoring the question. "What was he doing chasing that man, and handcuffing him, and then turning him over to the police. Is Fox a cop, too? Is he a plainclothes detective or something?"

"Whoa, there," Paula said, laughing. She took Cindy's arm and steered her in the direction of the parking lot where her car awaited them. "One thing at a time. First of all, Fox isn't a cop; he's a bounty hunter."

Cindy stopped walking. "A bounty hunter! I thought they only existed in Westerns."

"Well, Council Rock has at least one. Fox goes after and apprehends bail jumpers."

"People waiting for trial who flee jurisdiction and forfeit their bail?" Cindy asked, falling into step alongside Paula again.

"Right. In return for bringing them back he collects a fee, which is a percentage of the set bail."

"I see. So the higher the bail, the more money he makes."

Paula nodded as they approached her car. "That's why I was surprised to see him chasing down that guy today. He looked like a petty crook, and Fox doesn't usually waste his time on them. But he was doing it for Sheriff Tully. He's another Seminole, and they're pretty tight."

"I *thought* he was Indian," Cindy said softly, as Paula unlocked her door and walked around to the driver's side.

"Half," Paula corrected. "His mother was a tourist from up North. But in his mind, his attitudes, his approach to life, Fox is all Indian."

They got into the car, and Paula started the motor and drove off, pulling onto the main road which led out of town.

"You said he usually doesn't bother with small-time criminals," Cindy went on, pursuing the subject. "He mainly chases the big ones, organized crime figures, people like that?"

"Anybody with a big price tag attached," Paula replied. "He's the best at what he does, and the cops call him in on the toughest cases, the ones they can't crack. He goes out of state a lot, sometimes even out of the country. He went down to Mexico a few months back, after some drug kingpin, finally tracked him to Guadalajara, Johnny told me. Fox must have picked up a nice piece of change for that one."

"He ought to buy himself a new truck," Cindy commented, smiling. "The one he has looks like it's about to disintegrate."

Paula shook her head. "He loves that old piece of junk, fixes it himself." Paula craned her neck at an intersection and then gunned the motor. "Fox is hard to understand. Johnny says he has expensive equipment, a whole roomful of computers—some of them tied in to the government banks—to assist in his investigations, but he'll drive that raggedy pickup until it collapses into a heap of rubble. He just doesn't seem to care much about anything but his work."

"He sounds like an independent type," Cindy said.

"Oh, he is that, all right. He's descended from a long line of renegade Seminoles who chose to stay in Florida and live as hunters and fishermen rather than accept reservation life in the West. His father and grandfather made their living from the land."

"What happened to his mother?" Cindy asked.

Paula glanced at her quickly, then looked back at the road. "She left him with his father and went back North. His father's family raised him." She paused and added, "He's illegitimate. The story goes that his mother viewed his father as a good time, a little distraction during her vacation. She discovered she was pregnant and had the child up North, returning just long enough to leave the baby here—deposit him on the Fox doorstep, so to speak. As far as I know they never saw her again."

"How horrible for him," Cindy said softly, thinking of the green eyes, surely the stamp of his absent mother.

"Yeah, I guess it must have been pretty rough, being a half-breed in a Southern town, and a bastard to boot. He was pretty much of a hell-raiser when he was a kid. My brother Johnny wasn't supposed to play with him."

"Because of his background?" Cindy asked, dismayed at such prejudice toward an innocent child.

"No. Because he was always in trouble. My grandmother used to call him 'that desperado' and told Johnny that she would box his ears if she saw him with

Drew. Which only made Johnny anxious to tag after him at every opportunity."

"Desperado," Cindy repeated, laughing. "Isn't that a little dramatic?"

"Well, she was Spanish, you know, given to colorful expressions in her native language. She also called my father 'that gringo' until the day she died, at which point my parents had been married for thirty years."

"Where is Johnny now?" Cindy inquired.

"Up in Atlanta. My father got him a job when my parents moved there. It was during our junior year, remember?"

"I remember. So you're the only one of your family left in this area now."

"Yup," Paula said, pulling into the driveway of an apartment complex. "I wanted to come back here when we graduated; this place will always be home to me. And Johnny looks Fox up every time he comes to visit me. They were great friends."

"Fox was raised by his father's family, then?"

"Until he was sixteen. He left home then, taking a number of lunatic jobs until he found his calling."

"Lunatic jobs?"

"Jobs only a lunatic would take. He has a natural cunning and amazing agility, so he always wound up doing things nobody else would try. Johnny told me about some of his adventures."

"Such as?" Cindy asked curiously, as Paula pulled into a reserved parking space in front of an ultra-modern brick building.

Paula sent her an arch glance. "He fascinates you, doesn't he?"

"Answer the question."

Paula chuckled, shutting off the motor. "Let's see. He was a bonded courier for a while, those guys with briefcases handcuffed to their wrists and pistols in their shoes."

"Briefcases full of diamonds, you mean."

"Right. He got shot doing that, so he switched to something safer, high-rise construction work, teetering on six-inch girders five stories above the ground."

Cindy burst out laughing.

"But that was too dull, I guess, because the next thing I heard, he was riding shotgun on armored trucks transporting government payrolls."

"Good lord," Cindy said, shaking her head.

"So you can see how his training and experience were perfectly suited to his current occupation. He can go his own way, work when he wants to, and slake his thirst for adventure at the same time." Paula gestured expansively at the building before them. "El Rancho Desmond, the second floor of it anyway. Let me help you take your luggage out of the trunk."

Each of the women took a bag, and Cindy followed Paula up an exterior flight of stone steps. They passed the potted palms flanking the entrance and went through glass doors, which admitted them to the first floor landing. The air inside was blessedly cool. Paula led the way up an additional series of carpeted stairs to her apartment.

"This is it," she announced, unlocking the door and hefting Cindy's suitcase over the threshold. "I was on a waiting list six months to get this place."

"It's lovely," Cindy said, looking around at the luxurious apartment. A living room with a cathedral ceiling and a balcony overlooking the street opened into a dining area with a mirrored wall facing them and a gleaming galley kitchen with all the latest appliances. A hall led away from the living room to the bedrooms at the back. The whole place was done in pleasant neutral tones: beige carpeting, furniture and draperies in cocoa, sand and taupe, with warm accents of orange and peach in the throw pillows and in the modern paintings on the walls. "How does a humble nurse afford a place like this?"

"She doesn't," Paula replied. "I am also the assistant manager of the complex, for which I get a considerable break on the rent. I collect checks, take complaints, and serve as general dogsbody for the outfit that owns the buildings."

"I see."

Paula dropped what she was carrying and headed for the kitchen. "You should have seen this apartment before I took it. I was so anxious to get in here I agreed to take on the mess. I needed two weeks to clean it up before I could move in."

"It was dirty?" Cindy asked, fingering a china cat on an end table.

"Not exactly. The person who lived here before me had some rather unusual decorating ideas. The walls in the living room were black. When you pulled the drapes closed it was like a full blackout during the London blitz. And as if to make up for that, the master bedroom was fluorescent green, and there were orange flowers all over the bathroom walls.''

"Oh, dear.''

"I almost went blind when the real estate agent showed it to me. I had it all stripped and painted before I brought one stick of furniture through the door.'' She pointed to the back of the apartment, at the same time poking around in the freezer for ice. "Just put your things in the guest room on the left.''

Cindy picked up the bag Paula had dropped and lugged her things down the hall, her sandals noiseless on the thick carpeting. The spare bedroom had a single bed with a brass bedstead, covered with a multicolored quilt. It was on the same side of the building as the balcony, which ended about three feet from its window. Cindy dumped her bags on the bed and removed her shoes, wiggling her bare toes blissfully on the cool rug. She ambled back out to the kitchen, where Paula was mixing a pitcher of iced tea.

"It's instant,'' she said to Cindy, when she saw her watching the process. I can't be bothered boiling the water for the real stuff. It's probably full of additives which will kill us both, but today I'm too hot to care.''

"Has Andrew Fox always lived in this area?'' Cindy asked, leaning on the counter which bordered the dining area.

"Back to him, are we?'' Paula said, grinning. "I can see that he made quite an impression. Well, he usually does.''

Cindy merely stared at her until she shrugged and said, "He travels a lot, as I said, but his home base has always been Council Rock. He's very close to his father's family, but almost nobody else." She smiled as she emptied a tray of ice into the plastic pitcher. "He used to live in a lean-to on his uncle's property, if you can believe that. Then he had an apartment, and now he's moved into one of those waterfront condominiums on the other side of town. They cost a fortune, and his change of lifestyle has occasioned quite a bit of comment around town. There's a lot of speculation about his reasons for relocation. It's rather out of character."

"Why should it seem unusual?" Cindy inquired. "After all, he must make a lot of money doing what he does; you said so yourself."

Paula took two tall glasses down from a cupboard and filled them, shaking her head. "That's not the point. If you knew Fox better, you would know he'd never buy such a place for himself."

Cindy didn't respond, mulling that over. She accepted her glass from Paula's hand and drank deeply, pulling her blouse loose from the waistband of her skirt.

"Do you mind if I take a shower?" she said to Paula. "I'm a little grimy from the trip."

"Be my guest. There are towels in the bathroom closet and a robe on the back of the door."

Cindy went into the bathroom and started to strip. As she removed her blouse she noticed that there was a crusted scab just below the short sleeve. The blood had congealed into an irregular mass on the inside of her arm.

She had felt no pain at all. She must have been cut when the window broke.

Shrugging her shoulders philosophically, she took off the rest of her clothes and got into the shower, turning on the taps and adjusting the flow of water. As she washed the cut it began to bleed again and to sting. Annoyed, she finished her ablutions hurriedly and belted the terry robe around her, wadding up some tissue paper and holding it to the cut. Barefoot and dripping, she padded out to find Paula, who was pressing a white uniform on a portable ironing board set up in the living room.

"Look at this," Cindy said, extending her arm. "I didn't even know the darn thing was there, and now it's bleeding all over the place."

Paula unplugged the iron and moved to take a closer look. "Son of a gun," she marveled. "That must have happened this afternoon. You mean to tell me you didn't even feel it?"

"Nope. I didn't even know it was there until I took off my blouse."

Paula winked. "Too dazzled by Mr. Andrew Fox, no doubt."

Cindy sighed. "Do you have a Band-Aid or something?"

"What, are you kidding? You're talking to Nurse Nancy here. I've got the works on hand at all times for just such emergencies. Have a seat and I'll be right there. I'll only charge my evening rates. That's a reduced fee."

"Very comforting," Cindy said, settling on the edge of the couch and watching warily as Paula produced a zippered bag from the hall closet.

"First, antiseptic," Paula announced, kneeling in front of her on the floor. "I love to show off for my friends," she confided in a lower tone, as she daubed the wound with something from a bottle that looked evil and smelled worse.

"Ouch," Cindy exclaimed, pulling her arm back.

"Still a sissy, I see," Paula remarked, taping a patch of gauze in place over the cut. "Remember that time in college when you fell from the ledge outside the boys' dorm? You moaned about your sprained ankle for the rest of the semester."

"You're lucky it wasn't broken," Cindy responded sourly. "That's what I get for going to rescue you when you got stuck up there. I wanted no part of that escapade, if you remember."

"Pick, pick, pick," Paula said cheerfully, recapping the bottle and straightening up. "You have to admit that if not for me your college years would have been far less colorful."

"Far more productive, you mean," Cindy countered, standing and admiring Paula's neat, professional handiwork.

"You're the one who made the dean's list every marking period," Paula called from the hall. "I couldn't have done that much damage." She walked back into the living room, glancing at her watch. "My turn in the bathroom," she added. "I've got the night shift at the hospital tonight, 7:00 PM to 3:00 AM, and I'm running late." She waved her hand, encompassing the apartment. "Make yourself at home. The refrigerator is full of food; the TV and stereo are self-explanatory. Just make sure you answer the phone because I have to take tenant messages. There's a pad next to the phone; write down the name and apartment number of anybody who calls and the complaint. The messages are usually complaints." She grinned, and then vanished down the hall. Seconds later Cindy heard the rushing water of the shower.

She wandered back into her room and fished out some old clothes to wear, things in which she would be comfortable while studying. She planned on spending the evening profitably, organizing her notes. When Paula emerged fifteen minutes later, dressed for work, Cindy was already unpacking her briefcase on the dining room table.

"Look at you," Cindy said, smiling at Paula's transformation. In her white nylon pantsuit and sensible shoes, she was a model of decorum. "Even your hair looks starched."

"It is," Paula replied. "It wilts like lettuce in this humidity unless I use a can of hairspray on it." She picked up her purse and car keys from the counter. "Are you sure you'll be all right here?"

"For heaven's sake, Paula, what can happen? Go to work."

Paula nodded, then peered at the cover of the book Cindy held. "What are you reading?"

"*Aboriginal Legends of the North American Indians*," Cindy recited, not looking up.

"Um," Paula said. "Sounds yummy. Save it for me, but don't tell me the ending."

Cindy raised her eyes.

"Okay, okay, I'm going. I'll try not to wake you up when I come home." She waved and then left, locking the door behind her.

Cindy worked in silence for two hours, interrupted only once by a phone call. She left a note for Paula saying that Mr. Axelrod in 12-C wished to inform her that his bathtub was leaking, and would she please contact the plumber. She was thinking about making coffee and taking a break when the doorbell rang at about nine-thirty.

Cindy got up to answer it, taking care to look through the peephole before she threw the bolt.

Andrew Fox was standing in the hall.

Her heart beating a little faster, Cindy opened the door.

He leaned against the jamb and folded his arms.

"Hi, Lucinda," he said quietly. "Remember me?"

Two

Cindy was silent, painfully conscious that her hair was screwed into a straggling bun on the top of her head and that there was a badly chewed pencil stuck in it. She was also barefoot and wearing ancient, paper-thin jeans faded to white at the seams. These were topped by a bleach-spotted sweatshirt bearing the slogan: "Run for Life—The 1983 Juvenile Diabetes marathon." Why, just once, couldn't she be wearing a black lace negligee when an attractive man appeared unexpectedly? Or at least a cocktail dress with high heels. But no. On such occasions she was invariably attired in the most ragged, ridiculous clothes she owned. It seemed to be a curse from which there was no escape.

He shook his head. "No response," he mourned. "How quickly they forget."

Cindy snapped out of it. "Of course I remember you," she said, recovering.

"Good." They stared at each other. "Well," he went on, "do I stand out here in the hall like a student selling magazines?"

"I'm sorry, come in. Please excuse me. I just wasn't expecting anyone." She stepped aside and he walked past her into Paula's apartment.

"Paula's not home," she said, watching as he looked around.

His light eyes moved back to her face. "I know that. I came to see you."

Cindy's pulse jumped. "Oh, yes?"

"Nice place," he commented. "Last time I saw it, it was a mess."

"When was that?"

"A couple of days before Paula moved in. She was having it painted, and Johnny and I carried some stuff up for her. He was here for a visit." He eyed her levelly. "Paula didn't seem to know what to do with me. I think she was afraid I was going to set a signal fire on the balcony."

This so accurately described Paula's attitude toward him that Cindy couldn't suppress a giggle. He smiled at her response.

The telephone rang, interrupting their shared moment. Cindy moved to get it, took the message for Paula and hung up. She glanced around for a pencil with which to write it down. Fox stepped in front of her and removed the mangled pencil from her hair.

"Looking for this?" he asked mildly.

"Thank you," Cindy said briskly, as if she had placed it there for safekeeping. This attitude was a little difficult to maintain as her hair, loosened by his action, tumbled from its confinement and fell over her right eye, obscuring her vision. Coughing delicately, she shoved it unceremoniously behind her ear, scribbling quickly.

"Lucinda, Lucinda, let down your hair," Fox recited softly.

"I didn't let it down, it fell down. Besides, that line is supposed to be for Rapunzel." She tossed pencil and pad onto the telephone table.

"A princess by any other name..." he said, shrugging.

"I'm not a princess."

He nodded wisely. "Oh, yes, you are. Take it from me. I can spot a princess a mile off, Lucinda."

"Please stop calling me that," she said faintly. "It makes me feel like I'm back in fourth grade, being called on the carpet by one of the nuns."

"Okay. Cindy it is," he replied, chuckling.

Annoyed at her loss of composure, Cindy gathered her hair in her hands, planning to bind it up again. Standing there facing him with it falling about her face made her feel childish and awkward.

He saw her intention and stayed her hand, closing his strong brown fingers around her wrist. "Don't do that," he said quietly. "Your hair is so pretty, such a nice color, not too yellow and not too red. What do you call that shade?''

''Strawberry blonde,'' Cindy replied, swallowing, intensely aware of his touch.

''It looked beautiful this afternoon, like a beacon in that dull street, a river of light flowing over your shoulders.'' His hand moved to touch the strands lying against her neck, and his fingertips brushed her skin.

Cindy closed her eyes. She had to put him at a distance, fast. She was definitely getting out of her depth.

She stepped back, away from him. ''Do you always pay such extravagant compliments to women you've just met?'' she asked frostily.

He hung his head, clasping his hands behind his back and staring at the floor. ''I think I've just been put in my place,'' he said, sighing dramatically. His mocking tone and exaggerated attitude of contrition had the desired effect on Cindy: her high-handedness became ridiculous in her own eyes. She was beginning to see that it was impossible to gain the advantage with him. The best she could hope for was a draw.

''Look, Mr. Fox,'' she said evenly, deciding to try the forthright approach, ''suppose you tell me why you came here.''

''Drew,'' he corrected, dropping his chastened schoolboy act and resuming his normal stance.

''Drew,'' she repeated dutifully.

''Actually,'' he said, ''I came here to apologize.''

Cindy frowned, puzzled. ''Apologize for what?''

''For your injury. I stopped off at the hospital tonight and Paula fixed me up.'' He touched the neat patch of gauze that had replaced his makeshift dressing. "She told me you got cut too, and I feel responsible."

"Don't be silly," Cindy said, turning away. "It's nothing."

"I'll be the judge of that. Let me see."

Cindy thrust her arm behind her back.

He shook his finger in her face. "Let me see it, princess, or I'll turn you over my knee."

He seemed ready to do just that, so Cindy offered the hidden arm reluctantly.

Fox took her hand and pushed the sleeve back from her wrist, turning her arm over to see the inside. He gently probed the edges of the bandage, his touch firm and sure.

"No redness, no swelling. And another nifty wrapping job by Paula Desmond, R.N." He looked up to meet her eyes. "I guess you'll be okay."

"I told you I was all right," Cindy responded huffily, trying to pull her hand from his.

"Wait a minute," he cautioned. "Not so fast." Before she could react he raised her trapped fingers to his lips.

"What are you doing?" Cindy gasped.

"Isn't it obvious?" he murmured, his mouth caressing her hand.

"No, it's not," she replied, tugging harder, but to no avail.

"I'm kissing it to make it well," he said softly, trailing his tongue along her knuckles.

"My arm was cut, not my hand," she said logically, trying to hang on to some shred of sanity. The moist warmth of his mouth was traveling up her arm like an electrical current.

"I'll kiss that, too," he responded, his lips moving past her wrist.

"Stop!" she cried, in a voice so loud and anxious that he obeyed her, surprising both of them. He released his hold, and she scrambled backward, her eyes wide.

"Are you afraid of me?" he asked, alarmed. He hadn't intended to scare her.

Cindy didn't know what to say. Fear didn't exactly describe what she felt.

Fox watched her, his light eyes vivid, almost otherworldly in his dusky face. His black hair shone like polished ebony in the artificial light, and the white bandage stood out against it like a lonely patch of snow on dark macadam. In his tight jeans and loose cotton shirt, his expression alert, but patient, he looked like the modern embodiment of one of his ancient ancestors, who knew how to wait and listen.

"Just don't . . ." Cindy said, leaving the sentence unfinished but gesturing to indicate that he should stand back.

"I won't," he replied, in a low tone. He knew better than to push her in this mood.

Cindy took a deep, shaky breath. He waited until she met his gaze directly and then said, "I didn't mean to upset you. Please allow me to make amends. Let me take you to dinner on Saturday night, that is if you have nothing else planned."

Cindy heard herself saying, as if by rote, "I have nothing else planned."

"Then you'll go?" he asked, searching her face as if waiting for her to change her mind.

She nodded dumbly.

He smiled, his white teeth flashing against his brown skin. "Do you like seafood?"

"Why, yes. I do."

"Fine. I know a place, Neptune's Table, down in St. Petersburg Beach. It's about a twenty-minute ride. Would that be all right?"

"Okay," she said. Anything would be all right.

"I'll pick you up around seven-thirty." He moved toward the door, intent on getting out before she called back her acceptance.

"All right."

He stopped, smiled back at her, and then made a hasty exit. Cindy remained in the same spot for about a minute, trying to absorb what had just happened. Then she went into the bathroom and looked at herself in the mirror.

Her features were the same: straight nose, full mouth, large blue eyes, complemented by pale skin and red-gold hair. But she felt different.

"You have a date with a bounty hunter," she said to the girl in the glass, and then she shook her head.

She must be losing her mind.

When Paula unlocked the apartment door at three-forty in the morning, Cindy was sitting on the sofa, an unread book open in her lap.

"You still up?" Paula asked wearily. "Those aboriginal legends must be more riveting than I thought."

"That's not it," Cindy answered, as Paula slung her purse into a chair and slipped off her shoes. "Drew Fox was here. He asked me to dinner on Saturday night."

Paula whistled. "Boy. I must say he's living up to his reputation as a fast worker. What did you say?"

"Yes."

Paula shook her head. "I can't understand you. In school you always thought I was too wild; you had to be coaxed along to do anything. And now here you are dating the local heartbreaker, totally unfazed by all the stories I told you about him."

"I'm not unfazed by them, or by him. As a matter of fact, I find him completely unnerving. But I like him."

"Of course you do. *Everybody* likes him; he's a charmer." Paula unbuttoned her collar and ran her fingers through her hair. "Listen, kiddo, you're talking to a veteran of that particular war. I had a monster crush on him the whole time I was in high school, when he was friends with Johnny. But his track was too fast even for me, and he runs it alone." She peered at Cindy's face, which was closed. "Okay, that's all I'm going to say. You're a big girl, you have to make up your own mind."

"I have. And I will."

Paula turned her hands out, palms up, in a gesture of surrender. "Did he say where you were going?"

"Some place in St. Petersburg Beach—Neptune's Locker."

"You mean Neptune's Table?"

"That's it."

Paula nodded. "What clothes did you bring? That's a pretty fancy restaurant."

Cindy looked stricken. "All I have are jeans and a few skirts. I wasn't expecting an active social life. What will I wear?"

"Something of mine, I guess. In college that was your usual solution to such a problem."

Cindy made a face at her. "You forced those clothes on me because you said I was never dressed right."

"You never were. On the rare occasions that you went out at all you always looked like you were ready for a hot date in the reference stacks."

"But the sharing was always your idea, right?" Cindy said slyly.

"Right," Paula agreed wearily, aware of what was coming.

"Then you can hardly blame me for your *generous* impulses, dear," Cindy replied. She brightened. "Got any silk dresses?"

"Let's take a look," Paula said resignedly, and they went together to her bedroom to ransack the closet.

Cindy tried to keep her mind occupied until Saturday came, but found it a difficult task. Her thoughts kept wandering from her work to Andrew Fox and their brief but telling interlude in Paula's apartment.

She and Paula had found a suitable dress among Paula's things, a peach silk jersey shift that flattered Cindy's coloring. It was sleeveless, with a low neckline and a shirred hem that just covered her knees. With her high-heeled sandals and appropriate jewelry, Cindy was confident that she would look right for the occasion.

Paula was off Saturday night and had a date also, with a pharmacist who worked in the hospital dispensary. They were going to a rodeo, a prospect that Paula deemed questionable at best, but she liked the guy and was determined to tough it out.

"What do you think?" Paula asked, pausing in the doorway to Cindy's room. Cindy looked up from the task of examining her panty hose for snags. Paula was dressed in cowboy boots, a tailored shirt with black piping, and western-cut jeans; she had a red bandanna tied around her neck. "Too Dale Evans?"

"More like Annie Oakley," Cindy replied, getting up to look for her bottle of hand lotion.

The telephone rang as she was coming out of the bathroom.

"Will you get that?" Paula called from her bedroom. "It's probably Mr. Axelrod about his bathtub again. His apartment should be floating like the Ark by now. Tell him the plumber is on the way."

Cindy answered on the third ring.

"Hi," a masculine voice said, and she knew who it was. "Are we still set for tonight? This is Drew," he concluded, unnecessarily.

"Yes, unless you're calling to say something has come up and you can't make it," Cindy responded.

"Oh, no. I just wanted to tell you that the restaurant is on the marina, and it can get chilly there after the sun goes down, so you'd better bring a sweater."

"It was thoughtful of you to let me know."

"Yeah, well, I'll see you at seven-thirty, then, okay?"

"Okay."

There was a pause. Then, "Cindy, the sweater was an excuse. I really wanted to hear your voice, that's all. Look for me when the sun goes down. 'Bye."

"Goodbye." Cindy hung up reluctantly, wondering about his sudden admission.

"Who was that?" Paula asked, walking into the living room with her hairbrush in hand.

"Drew Fox. He wanted to tell me to bring a sweater because it gets cold near the water at night."

Paula raised her brows. "That was nice of him."

"You sound surprised."

Paula drew her mouth down at the corners. "Don't bait me. I merely made an observation." She headed back to her room, brushing her hair.

"Anyway, he said that wasn't the real reason he called. It was just a pretext."

Paula paused in mid-stroke. "What?"

"He said he just wanted to talk to me, hear my voice. Do you know I recognized his right away? All he said was hi, and I knew. And he didn't mistake me for you, either."

"'My ears have not yet drunk a hundred words of thy tongue's uttering, yet I know the sound,'" Paula recited, batting her eyelashes.

"Something like that," Cindy said, refusing to be cowed.

Paula shook her head, but wisely refrained from further comment. Cindy retreated to her bedroom to finish dressing, and their doors closed simultaneously, as if by mutual agreement.

Cindy was ready long before Fox was due, which was a mistake. She paced up and down the living room, wishing that Paula had not left earlier so that she would have someone to talk to in order to pass the time. When the doorbell finally rang she jumped, as if she hadn't been expecting it all along.

Fox was standing in the hall, wearing tan chinos with a light brown linen jacket and a pale green shirt. His silk tie blended perfectly with his clothes, but it looked as if it was choking him, and Cindy wondered how long it had been since he'd last worn one.

"Hi," he said. "You look nice. These are for you." He handed her a bouquet of flaming hibiscus, the color of an August sunset, which he'd been concealing behind his back.

"Thank you," Cindy said, accepting the flowers and going back inside to put them in water. He followed slowly, watching her.

"I wasn't expecting this," she said, rooting through the cupboards for a vase.

"I wasn't expecting it, either. But I passed a florist's, and I was thinking about you, so I just stopped and got them. But then, I've been thinking about you a lot these past few days. If I'd been passing a furniture store you probably would have wound up with a desk."

Cindy glanced at him quickly, and he grinned. She smiled back at him.

"How's your head?" she asked.

"Fine. How's your arm?"

"Fine."

"Then I guess we're both fine," he said, and she laughed.

Cindy left the flowers standing in an old milk bottle filled with water. She picked up her jacket and purse.

"Shall we dance?" he said, extending his arm.

She took it, and they walked out together.

Three

The Gulf Coast night was warm and fragrant, refreshed by a salt-laden breeze. Fox led Cindy to a late-model sports car standing next to the curb.

"This is your car?" she asked.

"Yes. You were expecting to go in the pickup?"

Cindy shrugged. "I guess I hadn't thought about it," she answered truthfully.

"Would you have minded that?" he asked as he opened the door for her, alert to her response.

"Why should I? It's transportation."

Fox thought that over while he walked around to get in on his side.

"You know," he said quietly, as he pulled onto the road, "when I called earlier I half expected you to say that you had changed your mind."

"Why?" Cindy asked, turning to look at him.

He lifted one shoulder slightly. "Ladies like you don't usually..."

"Keep their word?" Cindy inquired, an edge to her tone.

He shook his head. "I just don't go out with ladies like you a lot." He smiled, but his eyes didn't change. "Not much opportunity to meet refined young professors in my line of work."

"I'm not a professor yet," Cindy replied. Then she grinned at him. "Maybe I'm not even that refined."

"I'd have to argue that point with you," he said mildly. He turned to look directly at her. "Did Paula tell you that I'm a half-breed?" he asked suddenly.

Disturbed by the bluntness of his question, Cindy nevertheless answered him with the same candor.

"She didn't have to tell me. I knew it when we first met, from your eyes."

He examined her face briefly before turning his attention back to the road. "My parents were never married," he went on evenly. "My mother left me with my father right after I was born, and she went back to Boston."

"That must have been very hard for you," Cindy murmured. It sounded inane to her own ears, but she didn't know what he wanted to hear.

"Those who knew her say that I look like her, not in coloring so much, but in my features."

"Then she must have been very beautiful," Cindy said, meaning it, but also trying to make him feel better concerning a subject about which he was obviously very sensitive.

"And you have the nerve to suggest that you're not refined," he said, tossing her a teasing glance, and she smiled. She could almost feel the tension leave them like the passing of a dark cloud.

As Fox turned the wheel to negotiate an intersection, Cindy noticed a leather sheath strapped to his midsection.

"What's that?" she asked curiously, before she considered that the question might be rude.

"What?" he responded, watching the stream of cars moving in the opposite direction.

"That thing around your middle—looks like an eyeglass case or something."

"Oh. That's a bowie knife," he said casually.

"A bowie knife," she repeated in disbelief.

"Yeah. I don't like to carry a gun when I go out socially. My father taught me how to throw it."

He noticed her transfixed stare. "Relax, princess. I'm not going to throw it at you."

"Why do you have to carry anything at all?" she inquired, still trying to adjust to the idea.

"The people I take back to prison usually aren't too happy about it, or fond of me for getting them there. On occasion they've taken their revenge when I least expected it. Nobody stays in prison forever, you know." He glanced over at her. "I'll leave it in the car if it upsets you."

"Oh, no, no. I was just surprised, that's all." Cindy waited a moment, and then said, "How did you get started with what you're doing, Drew? If you don't mind telling me."

"I don't mind," he answered mildly. "I was always good at tracking, I learned to hunt animals when I was a kid. I never killed them—my family didn't believe in it—except for food, and we didn't need that. But I got a lot of experience following scents and clues, things an animal leaves behind that tell you where it has gone. And people are animals too, they leave spoor just like wildlife in the woods. At first, I just tracked down anybody who bolted and collected the money. But as I became better and better at it, the cops called me in to get people they couldn't catch."

"Paula says you go after big-time criminals now," Cindy observed.

"Oh, yes, I'm a member of the elite these days," he answered, with a hint of self-mockery. "As far as my job goes, anyway. They've got computers and radar devices and everything else to assist me."

"Who does?"

"Whoever I'm working for. I have some stuff of my own too, but the most sophisticated equipment is reserved for the police: state, feds, Interpol."

"What's Interpol?"

"International Police."

"Paula said you went to Mexico not long ago on a case."

"Paula says quite a bit, apparently," he commented dryly. "I hope she hasn't been scaring you off me."

"I'm here, aren't I?" Cindy replied defensively, and he smiled slightly.

"Yes, you are," he said quietly, and left it at that.

They approached Tampa Bay, and Fox pulled onto the causeway, which spanned the gleaming water like a thin ribbon. The bay fanned out from it on both sides, sparkling like an aquamarine in the fading light.

"This is so beautiful," Cindy breathed, craning her neck to look around her. "But the road is so low, doesn't it flood?"

"Wait until you see it on the way back, when it's dark, with a hundred lights reflecting in the water. And yes, it does flood, all the time during hurricane season. That's the reason the Sunshine Skyway was built so high, fifteen stories above the bay at its highest point. It connects St. Petersburg and Bradenton. There are signal lights on the ramparts to warn off planes."

Cindy shuddered. "I don't think I'd like to go on that," she said.

Fox glanced at her. "Afraid of heights?"

She nodded.

"Trust me, princess, I won't let you fall," he said softly, and Cindy felt a plummeting sensation in her stomach, as if she were tumbling from a cliff already. Maybe she was.

Fox drove through St. Petersburg down to the water, parking in the lot of a restaurant that flanked a marina. Small boats bobbed at anchor all around them as he led her up an entrance ramp designed to look like a gangway. Inside, the walls were floor-to-ceiling glass, affording an unobstructed view of the inlet.

"This is lovely, Drew," Cindy said, as the hostess led them to their table. "Thank you for bringing me here."

He eyed her speculatively for a few seconds, and then replied, "Thank you for coming with me."

They sat next to one of the windows, and Cindy studied the view as Fox consulted the menu.

"What body of water is this?" she asked, as a soft breeze drifted in through the screen and caressed her face.

"Boca Ciega Bay," he answered. He watched her rapt examination of the scenery, smiling to himself, and then suggested gently, "Would you like to look at this?" He handed her the tassled menu.

She glanced at it perfunctorily, reading through the elaborate descriptions of seafood dishes in growing confusion. When she looked up at him he was grinning.

"Want me to chose for both of us?" he asked. When she agreed eagerly, he laughed.

The steward came by, and Fox ordered white wine. He poured for her when it arrived, watching her reaction as she took the first sip.

"Okay?" he asked, and she nodded. Fox signaled to the steward that he could go.

When the waitress arrived, Fox ordered a platter of bluepoint oysters on the half shell as an appetizer and lobster tails for two. Cindy felt a little queasy about the oysters, but gamely decided to say nothing and give them a try.

"I've been telling you all about me," Fox said as the waitress left. "What about you? What does a graduate assistant do? Assist graduates?"

His teasing grin told her he was kidding. She described the way her research program worked, and added that her supervisor, Richard Caldwell, had to approve her paper before she could get her degree.

"Yeah?" Fox said, taking a sip of wine. "So where is he?" He looked around the room as if he expected to find Richard propped against the wall like a garden rake.

"He's still up at the university. I'll be mailing him copies of my work so he can keep track of what I'm doing."

Fox toyed with the silver sugar bowl on the table. "So what's the subject of your thesis?" he asked.

"Seminole legends," Cindy answered, watching his face to see the impact of this information.

His unusual eyes widened. "No kidding! Hey, I'll be your research project."

"You're only half Seminole," Cindy said, her lips twitching.

"I'll be half your research project," he shot back, laughing.

The oysters arrived, and Cindy eyed them warily.

"Seriously," Fox said. "My grandfather knows an awful lot about the old stories; I'm sure he could help you. Would you like to meet him?"

Cindy stared at him. "Do you mean it?" she asked breathlessly. This was a golden opportunity, the chance of a lifetime to get the inside track. Sometimes it was hard for her to get her subjects to talk.

"Of course I mean it," Fox replied, chuckling. He reached for the oysters and speared one with a tiny fork. "I have to go away this week, but I can take you out there next Saturday, if that would be okay."

"That would be wonderful," Cindy replied, trying to contain her excitement. This became easier instantly as Fox lifted an oyster to her lips.

"Try one," he said.

Cindy stared at the slimy, gray-blue object. "These are raw?"

"Completely."

"Not cooked at all?"

"Not at all," he said, observing her consternation with amusement. "First time, huh?"

"Yes."

"Come on, princess, eat up," he said, prodding her lower lip with the fork.

Cindy closed her eyes and opened her mouth. The oyster slid between her lips and down to the back of her throat, where it lodged like a basketball.

"Did you swallow it?" he asked, trying not to laugh.

Cindy shook her head mutely.

He grabbed a glass of water and held it to her lips. "Here, drink this, and sort of shoot it down with the flow."

Cindy obeyed, gasping as the offending tidbit slid down her throat. Her eyes teared, and she blinked rapidly.

"We'll consider that experiment a failure," he said dryly. He signaled the passing waitress. "Please bring the lady a shrimp cocktail," he said. He glanced at Cindy. "Okay?"

"Okay," she said, vastly relieved.

"Why didn't you tell me you didn't like oysters?" he asked gently, as she patted her lips delicately with a linen napkin.

"I never had them, as I said, so I thought I'd give them a try," she answered. "You go ahead, though, don't let me stop you."

Fox examined the remaining oysters doubtfully. "I'm not too thrilled with them myself, now," he said, and then looked up at her.

Cindy made a gagging face, and they both laughed.

"I would have thought you'd have a taste for oysters, with your background," he said, filling her glass again with wine.

"What do you know about my background?" Cindy asked him, amused.

"Nothing, but I can make some good guesses," he replied.

"Go ahead," Cindy said, taking a drink, enjoying the game.

"Okay. I would say that your daddy was a lawyer, an accountant, or a teacher. Am I right?"

"A professor of ancient history," Cindy responded.

"Same thing. And you were the perfect teacher's daughter. You studied hard and got good grades, and never, ever, disobeyed the rules."

"I liked school," she said quietly. "I still do."

"I'll bet you loved to read, to sit in your room and dream."

"Books are better friends than people, sometimes," she answered.

"I'm doing pretty well so far," he observed.

"Continue," she said, becoming a little uncomfortable. Her shrimp cocktail arrived, and she nibbled at the succulent, curved pieces as he went on.

"All right. You were an only child, and you kept to yourself. You liked to play alone, and when you got older, the friends you had, like Paula, sought you out rather than the other way around."

"I prefer a few good friends to a crowd. Is that what you mean?"

"Close enough. And you were the focus of the family, the little treasure coddled by your parents and kept from all harm."

"My family loved me, yes," she said tightly. "Did Paula tell you any of this?"

"I've never discussed you with Paula. I didn't have to. What you are is written all over you."

"I don't think I've ever been dissected before," Cindy said carefully. "I'm not sure I like it."

His brown hand covered her white one on the table. "Don't get mad, princess. I admire what you are. I envy the opportunities you have. Nobody will ever say to you: 'that's not yours, you can't have it, don't touch.'"

Cindy met his eyes. "Do people say that to you?"

He looked away. "Sometimes. Money can't buy everything, you know."

"It buys quite a bit," she said resentfully, piqued at his mocking description of her life. "I understand you have a brand-new condo on the water. That mustn't be too hard to take."

Fox was silent for a moment, swirling the wine in his glass and watching the play of the soft light in its depths. Then he said, "Five years ago, when I first started making good money, I did all the usual things. I got a fancy apartment, bought a Jaguar that cost twice as much as the car I have now, a motorcycle and a boat. I had plenty of pretty toys. Then when I realized I was becoming more interested in things than in people I sold them. The apartment had more alarms than a firehouse, and I decided that wasn't worth worrying about, either. I went back to Council Rock."

"Then why the new condo?" Cindy asked curiously.

He smiled mysteriously. "I'll tell you about that sometime," he said, as the lobster was deposited on the table before them.

"It must be wonderful to live right on the ocean," Cindy said dreamily.

"We are all drawn to the water," he said quietly. "We began there, and we know it. We come back with a sense of peace and fulfillment, like a traveler returning home."

"What a very Seminole thing to say."

His emerald eyes caressed hers across the distance that separated them. "You should know."

A band began to play dance music in the next room, a pleasant accompaniment to their meal. The lobster was delicious, and the wine was wonderful, light and crisp.

"Would you like anything else?" Fox asked, as she set down her fork.

"Oh, no. I couldn't eat another thing. Everything was fantastic."

"Except the oysters," he reminded her, smiling.

"I'm sure an oyster fan would have loved them," she said, and he grinned.

"Would you like to go outside for a while? There's a deck along the back, and a nice breeze."

"That would be lovely," Cindy said, standing up.

Fox pulled out her chair and spoke to their waitress as they passed. He led the way to the rear door, which opened onto a wooden platform above the water. The wind whipped her hair around her face and flattened her thin skirt against her legs.

"Too cold?" he asked, as she pulled her jacket closer around her.

"Not at all, it's delightful," she replied, lifting her chin and drinking in the sea air.

"Do you mind if I smoke?" he asked, and she shook her head. He extracted a pack of cigarettes from his breast pocket and lit one, dragging on it until the tip glowed. He leaned back against a mooring post and held out his arm to her. It seemed the most natural thing in the world to step into its circle, and when he pulled her against him, she couldn't resist. She relaxed into the curve of his shoulder, inhaling the clean, sharp scent of his skin.

The wind dropped off, as if to accommodate them, and became a whisper, gently touching them as it passed.

"I love it when it's like this," he murmured, his voice rumbling in his chest beneath her ear. "It reminds me of a poem I heard when I was in school, by some woman, I forget her name. In the last line she describes something that 'blows by like music'. That's the way this breeze is, like music heard from a distance, or the faint scent of flowers when you pass a stall."

"Sara Teasdale," Cindy sighed, slipping her arms around his lean waist.

"What?"

"That's the name of the lady who wrote the line you just quoted."

He laughed softly. "You *would* know that."

"You're not at all what I thought you would be," Cindy said suddenly, surprising herself.

"I don't know how to respond to that," he said. "What were you expecting?"

Cindy lifted her head to look up at him. He was smoking slowly, looking out across the water, one big hand splayed in the small of her back, his eyes narrowed against the sting of the smoke.

"Well, from Paula's description, I was expecting..."

"A bone-crushing Neanderthal?" he suggested sarcastically, glancing down at her.

Cindy didn't answer, snuggling against his chest again and closing her eyes.

"You must disregard much of what Paula says about me," Fox went on, as if she had agreed with what he said. "I'm not at my best around her. She has some preconceived ideas about me, and at times I can't resist fulfilling her expectations."

"Why?"

She felt him shrug. "Just to be perverse, I guess. I don't like being considered an uncivilized boor, some savage who just discarded his loincloth yesterday." He held her off and turned her chin up to look into her eyes. "You don't see me that way, do you?" he asked.

"No," she answered simply. He tucked her back into his arms and rocked her gently.

"How do you feel?" he asked, his voice low and husky. "Are you warm enough?"

"I'm warm and wonderful and perfect," she answered, sighing.

"Then I'm glad I asked," he said, the tug of laughter in his tone.

I must be drunk, Cindy decided. She was saying things she knew she shouldn't, but couldn't seem to make herself stop, or care.

He finished his cigarette, tossing the butt into a wire receptacle on the dock. The wind freshened again, and Cindy shivered.

"We'd better go in," he said, and she straightened reluctantly, not eager to lose the enchantment of his embrace. He kept one arm across her shoulders as they went back inside and didn't release her completely until she sat in her chair.

"Coffee?" he said.

"Um, yes."

"How about some dessert?"

"I don't think so. I'm stuffed."

He smiled. "Okay." He gave the order to the waitress and then leaned across the table, touching her face.

"That wind put roses in your cheeks," he said.

"Then I'm glad we went out. I'm usually too pale."

"Paleface," he said, and their eyes met.

"Does it matter?" she asked softly.

"Does it matter to you?" he countered, watching her closely.

"The only thing that matters to me is how I feel," she replied, her voice trembling.

"And how do you feel?" he asked quietly.

"Now?"

He nodded.

"Happy."

The coffee came, and they parted, sitting back to drink it. But the moment hung between them, and when he asked her to dance, she stood without replying, anxious to feel his arms around her again.

They came together the instant their feet hit the dance floor. Cindy clung to him, barely moving, as they drifted to the music in a world of their own. They danced until the band packed up for the night. As Fox released her and stepped back, her lips brushed his throat accidentally, and she felt his whole body tense. He drew a shaky breath, exhaling slowly.

"Time to go," he said ruefully. "They're going to be handing us brooms pretty soon."

They walked slowly back to their table, holding hands. Fox paid the bill and left a tip, then helped Cindy into her jacket.

Darkness enclosed them as they left the restaurant and headed back to his car. There were only a few left in the lot, and the starting motor sounded loud in the late night stillness.

"Looks like we shut the place down," Fox observed, pulling out of the parking space.

"I wish we could have stayed longer," Cindy said wistfully, and he laughed softly.

"Not unless you wanted to wash the dishes," he said.

"Don't make fun of me," Cindy answered. "It was a wonderful night, and I didn't want it to end."

"I'm not making fun of you, princess," he said, his tone changing. "You're just more honest than I am, I guess. I joke about my feelings, to hide them."

"You don't have to do that with me, Drew," she said.

"I'll remember that," he replied softly.

The trip back was a quiet one. They shared the companionable silence that falls between two people who know they don't have to fill it. The drive across the causeway was as gorgeous as promised, but too short. They were back at Paula's complex in what seemed like record time.

"I'll walk you to the door," Fox said, as he helped Cindy out of the car.

"You're going away this week?" Cindy asked him during the climb to Paula's apartment.

"Yes, out of town, on a job."

"Is it dangerous?" Cindy inquired.

He looked down at her. "No, of course not."

She smiled sadly. "You'd say that whether it was or not."

He didn't comment, and she knew she was right.

"I'll be back Saturday. I'll call you then, to arrange the visit to my grandfather. He doesn't get a lot of company these days."

"Will he see me?" Cindy asked anxiously.

"He'll see you, don't worry," Fox replied. "When I tell him there's a beautiful *shankree* girl dying to meet him, I don't think he'll require much persuasion."

"*Shankree*?"

"Not Seminole. Non-Indian."

"Oh." They stopped outside Paula's door, and Cindy unlocked it with the extra key Paula had given her. She turned to face Fox, her heart pounding.

"I want to kiss you," he said tightly. "Very much."

"Yes, oh yes," she whispered.

"But after the other night . . ." he began.

Cindy put a finger to his lips, and he kissed it. "I know you better now," she said.

"I think you know me too well already," he murmured, bending his head to hers.

The touch of his mouth was light, exploratory, then quickly became insistent as Cindy slipped her arms around his neck. Her hand crept into his hair, which flowed over her fingers like thick black silk. His lips took hers hungrily, moving, caressing, never still, until she was kissing him back just as avidly. Never before had she been filled with such a desire to cling and submit. His mouth traveled to her neck, her ears, as he reached behind her and pushed in the door.

"What are you doing?" she whispered against his lips.

"I'm too old to make love in hallways," he replied huskily, almost carrying her with him so that her feet barely touched the floor.

Once inside, he lifted her against the wall, pinning her between it and his body. She felt engulfed by him: his mouth that devoured hers, his hands that molded her waist and hips, his thighs that held her in a viselike grip. She couldn't move, and didn't want to.

"How do you feel *now*, princess?" he murmured, pulling her against him, running his hands down her back.

Her soft moan was his answer. When he lowered his head to kiss her throat, she threw her head back, exposing the tender flesh to his caress. His lips parted, and she felt the moist heat of his tongue trace her collarbone. His hands came up to grasp her shoulders, and he held her steady as he explored lower, laving the valley between her breasts made available by the scoop neckline of her dress. His readiness was all too apparent through the thin barrier of her clothes, and she felt her control going, chasing after his, which was already fleeing and almost gone. He groaned deeply, pushing her skirt up, and sought her mouth again, wildly, promising and asking for more.

Cindy knew she couldn't handle this; he was too primed, too close to carrying them both away. Summoning her last shred of willpower she tore her mouth from Fox's. He tried to kiss her still, his eyes closed, but she evaded him deftly. His eyes opened, the lush lashes lifting, and the silence hung between them, punctuated by their harsh, ragged breathing.

Cindy swallowed. "You have to go," she gasped.

He leaned in to her, his gaze smoky with passion. "Do you want me to go?" he asked lazily, knowing the answer.

"No," she whispered.

He bent his head. She pushed back on his shoulders, not hard, but firmly enough to show that she meant it.

"Please. These feelings are too new," she said, "and this is moving too fast, Drew. I have to think."

"One more kiss," he said, "and I'll go."

"One more kiss, and you'll never go," Cindy answered.

He relented, straightening and moving away from her. She arranged her disordered clothes, her glance averted.

"Hey," he said, tipping her chin up with a long brown forefinger, "you're not sorry?"

She shook her head, unable to look at him. "No, I'm...overwhelmed; I just need some time, that's all."

"How about a week? I'll see you Saturday?"

She clutched the lapels of his jacket, suddenly frightened. "You will be careful?" she said anxiously.

"I always am," he replied lightly, smiling.

"I mean it, Drew. If anything were to happen to you..." She let the sentence trail off, unable to complete it.

He pulled her into his arms, seeking only to comfort now. "Nothing is going to happen to me, princess." He released her, prodding her chin gently with his fist. "Buck up. A week isn't very long."

"Okay," she replied, her tone subdued.

"You won't run off with some passing stranger while I'm gone?" he asked, only half kidding.

"Oh, Drew, don't be ridiculous," Cindy answered, inexplicably near tears.

"All right. See you Saturday, then."

"Saturday," she echoed, and watched as, with a final wink, he slipped quietly through the door and was gone. Cindy sagged against it, feeling almost too weak to stand.

In the course of one evening, her whole life had changed.

Four

Cindy was in the bathtub when she heard Paula return about half an hour after Fox left. She belted her terry robe around her, padding out to the kitchen, where Paula was preparing a midnight snack.

"Want one?" Paula asked, looking up and brandishing a cracker in Cindy's direction. "Low salt, low sugar, low taste."

Cindy smiled slightly, shaking her head. Paula had been on a diet since the day Cindy had met her and was convinced that if she could just lose eight pounds she would lead armies and rule the world. Her conspicuous lack of success in this enterprise never daunted her; she was certain that her failure was due to a mere technical hangup in finding the right plan. The fact that nobody else thought she was overweight never affected her determination either. Eight pounds thinner, and she would be perfection.

"What are they?" Cindy asked, nodding to the box of biscuits on the table. "A new diet?"

"Yup. You eat nothing but these for the first five days. What do you think?"

"I think a nurse should know better."

Paula shot her a disgusted glance. "Just what I need, moral support." She eyed her friend critically. "So how was the big date?"

Cindy smiled mysteriously.

"Hmm," Paula commented. "Just remember that Drew isn't the noble hero in one of those legends you love to read. He's a modern guy with modern problems, no matter how mythic he looks."

"I think we've already covered this ground," Cindy replied quietly, folding her arms.

Paula threw up her hands. "Okay, okay. What's next on the agenda?"

"He's bringing me to meet his grandfather next weekend."

Paula looked impressed. "Really? He *must* like you. He's not much for mixing family and friends."

"Well, I think it's really more that he's doing me a favor. I told him the subject of my paper, and he said that his grandfather knows a lot about the old legends and might be able to help me."

Paula shrugged. "Still, he didn't have to volunteer, right?"

"Right," Cindy agreed, eager to get off the subject of Drew's idiosyncracies. She treasured the impression she had of him from their evening together and didn't want Paula to ruin it. "Did you like the rodeo?" she asked quickly.

"I'm not sure," Paula replied, popping another cracker into her mouth. "It was different, all right, but the whole place smelled like a stockyard."

"It *was* a stockyard, wasn't it?"

Paula thought that over. "I guess it was," she conceded, giggling. She gestured toward the kitchenette. "Do you want something to eat? I promise I won't restrict you to these sawdust wafers."

"No, no. I'm tired and I think I'll turn in."

"Okay. Good night."

Cindy was walking down the hall when Paula's voice stopped her.

"Cindy?"

Cindy looked over her shoulder.

"I didn't mean to discourage you about Drew. Good luck with him. Really. Somebody's bound to get through to him sooner or later, and maybe it will be you."

Cindy nodded slowly and then went on her way to bed.

On Monday, Cindy saw the department chairman at Gulf Coast University, who gave her the preliminary information she needed. He also gave her a pass to use the reference room in the library, where she spent the rest of the week, immersed in the extensive folklore section. But despite Cindy's best efforts to keep busy, the wait for the weekend was interminable. She kept wondering where Drew was and what he was doing, if he was safe. It was ridiculous, because he'd been courting danger long before he met her and had managed to survive, but she couldn't dismiss the nagging feeling that he might be in trouble.

Saturday finally arrived. Cindy was up early, unable to sleep, and was making coffee in the kitchen when the doorbell rang at seven-fifteen. Yawning, Cindy wondered who might be calling at that hour, but when there was no response from Paula's room she shuffled to the door in her nightgown and slippers.

Drew was standing in the hall, rumpled and weary in jeans, boots, and a wrinkled navy T-shirt. He looked about to pass out on his feet, and he was the most beautiful sight Cindy had ever seen.

"Hello, princess," he said, his voice low and husky. He opened his arms.

Without a second thought, Cindy rushed into them.

He caught her to him and lifted her off her feet, swinging her in a half circle. With her arms around his neck and her eyes closed, Cindy drank in his presence like a heady draught.

"You feel wonderful," he murmured, his big hands caressing her body through the thin material of her gown. "I missed you."

"I missed you, too," she whispered, reaching up to touch his hair, her head still pressed to his shoulder. "I'm sorry I'm not dressed, I didn't expect you so early."

He laughed, withdrawing slightly to look down into her face. "I would have been earlier still, but I didn't think Paula would appreciate a visitor at three o'clock in the morning."

"What?"

He ran his finger along the bridge of her nose. "I've been sitting in the truck across the street since then, and I fell asleep." He bent to kiss her forehead. "I should have gone back home to clean up but I couldn't wait to see you."

Paula emerged from her bedroom, shrugging into her robe. She paused when she saw Drew.

"I thought I heard voices," she said. "Hi, Drew. Have you taken over the morning paper route?"

He grinned at Paula, and even though it was directed at her, Cindy could feel the force of his charm.

"Sorry, short stuff. I just wanted to see your roommate. Didn't mean to wake you."

"Well, this is touching, I must say," Paula observed dryly. "Care to stay for breakfast?"

"No, got to get home and change." He looked at Cindy. "I'll be back for you around nine, would that be okay?"

"Fine," she said, watching him move toward the door.

"So long, Paula." His voice dropped an octave. "See you later, princess." The door shut behind him and he was gone.

The silence lengthened as the sound of his footsteps faded down the corridor. The percolator steamed as it finished the coffee, and Paula helped herself to a cup of it before she said quietly, "He's quite taken with you, isn't he?"

"I hope so."

Paula sipped thoughtfully. "I originally thought that this was sort of a one-sided thing. I thought you were fascinated with Drew because he seemed to embody those traits you find so attractive in his culture. But it's more, isn't it?" She shook her head. "I've never seen him look so... smitten. And showing up here, at this hour, just to talk to you...." She let the sentence trail off and then cleared her throat. "So where does his grandfather live?" she asked brightly, changing the subject.

"I don't know. Don't you?"

"Not any more. When we were kids Drew's family lived in the old shantytown near the river, but I heard he moved them all out once he began to make some money. His father's dead now, but he still has some cousins and aunts in addition to the old man."

"And he supports all of them?" Cindy asked.

"As far as I know. He helps out, anyway, even if he doesn't keep them entirely. I know a couple of his younger cousins have jobs in town, and one of them is in college. He's probably paying for that too."

"He's very generous with them, isn't he?" Cindy asked softly.

"But not, I think, with many others," Paula replied meaningfully, and Cindy was still considering that statement as she removed the bread from the keeper and started breakfast.

When Drew returned he still looked tired, but his clothes were fresh and his hair was combed neatly, something she had rarely seen during the time she knew him. Though cut in a fashionably layered style, his hair was so thick and soft that it flew into bangs and wings around his ears as soon as he moved his head.

"Do I look all right?" Cindy asked nervously, gesturing to her denim skirt and short-sleeved sweater.

"Of course you look all right; you look lovely," he answered, laughing. "Why do you ask?"

"Well, I'm meeting your grandfather."

"It's my grandfather, Cindy, not the Emir of Katmandu," Drew responded dryly, shutting the door of Paula's apartment behind them.

"I want to make a nice impression," Cindy said, smoothing her skirt.

He stopped walking and turned her to face him. "How could you do anything else?" he asked quietly, and she dropped her eyes, touched beyond words.

"Now come along and stop fussing," he said briskly, bypassing the awkwardness of her reaction. "I hope you don't mind my bringing the truck, but it's better on some of the roads than the car."

"Is it difficult to get there?" Cindy asked as they descended the steps to the outside door.

"Not really, but it's a dirt track for about the last two miles. My grandfather resisted moving to a new house for a long time, but when it became clear that the move was necessary he agreed only on the condition that it be built in the woods. It isn't exactly the Glades, but I bought the property on a lake near my uncle's spread, and the climate is about the same."

"The reservations are in the south, aren't they?"

"Yes, but my people never lived on one," he answered proudly.

"Have you seen them?" Cindy asked, aware that she was venturing into dangerous territory, but so thirsty for his thoughts that she took the risk.

"I've seen Big Cypress, not Dania or Brighton," he answered, glancing at her as they walked toward his truck.

"What is Big Cypress like?"

"It's a swamp," he said bitterly. "You don't think the government would give good land to a bunch of Indians, do you?"

"But it's reclaimed, and arable, isn't it? I thought that was a provision of the treaty."

He paused next to the door on the passenger side of the cab and looked down at her.

"I forgot for a moment that you're an expert," he said, smiling narrowly.

"Hardly that," Cindy responded. "But I know something about Seminole history. It goes hand in hand with studying the literature."

Fox took her hand to help her up into the cab. He didn't reply to her statement, and she thought he had dropped the subject, until he slid behind the wheel. "Tell me what you know," he said flatly.

Cindy thought for a moment before she spoke. "The Seminoles are Creeks who migrated from Georgia and Alabama to Florida. The word 'Seminole' means 'runaway' in Creek. They lived in the Everglades and surrounding areas peacefully until, in the 1800's, they started harboring escaping slaves.''

"We have always loved freedom," Fox responded softly, starting the motor and guiding the truck into the stream of morning traffic.

"In 1817 Andrew Jackson invaded Seminole territory, on the pretext of tracking down fugitive slaves, and used that excuse to decimate the Indians. It was the costliest Indian war in U.S. history. Seven generals failed to conquer the tribe, which never surrendered."

His green eyes sought hers briefly, and then returned to the road. "You're well-informed," he commented quietly.

"I became fascinated with the history when I began studying the folk tales," Cindy admitted. "How could anyone fail to sympathize with the plight of such a brave, independent people?"

"Quite a few of your compatriots failed to sympathize with them at the time," he said tightly, his strong brown fingers tightening on the wheel.

Cindy felt her stomach muscles knotting. "You can't blame all of us for that, Drew," she said evenly, trying not to betray her emotion. "Would it be fair for me to hate present-day Englishmen because their ancestors starved mine during the potato famine?"

He sighed heavily, pulling to a stop at a red light. "Sorry," he said huskily, reaching over to cover her hand with his. She smiled at him, and the bad moment passed.

"I'm curious as to why your family is still in Florida," Cindy said, daring to breathe again. "Weren't most of the Seminoles removed to Oklahoma during the westward development? The 'Trail of Tears,' it was called, because so many died."

Fox nodded. "All but about fifteen hundred left for the West. The Foxes are part of the group that remained. They never gave up, and they never left."

"Paula said something about that." She studied his profile as the light changed and they moved forward again. "So I guess you're a renegade, huh?" she asked him.

He lifted a hand off the wheel and pointed his forefinger at her. "There's another theory about the origin of the word 'Seminole.' Have you ever heard it?"

Cindy searched her mind. "I don't think so."

"It comes from the time when the Spanish ruled in Florida, before Jackson and company took over. The story goes that Seminole is a corruption of the Spanish word 'Cimarron.' Know what it means?"

Cindy shook her head.

"Wild," he said, and grinned at her. She believed him.

"Did you really live in a lean-to?" Cindy asked suddenly, remembering something else Paula had said.

He took a left and headed out of town for the open road. "It wasn't a lean-to, it was a *chiksee*."

"One of those open houses used in the Everglades?"

He shot her an admiring glance. "Right. I wanted to see if I could build one from the ground up, and when I got finished I liked it so well I lived there for a while.

The *chiksee* is very well adapted to Florida weather, with a raised floor and a roof of bark and palmetto leaves. But it got kind of buggy in the hot weather and I eventually traded it in for an apartment." He laughed softly. "I guess I don't have the stoic endurance of my forebears."

"You must share my fatal weakness for air conditioning," Cindy commented, and he laughed again.

They were traveling on a thin strip of paved road through the scrub pines and date palms that comprise most of the vegetation of northern Florida. Occasionally a cypress would sweep its lacy tresses to the ground, creating a cool pocket of shade within its drooping branches, but the landscape was mostly covered by the tough cow grass that could survive for long periods without water. Cindy opened the top button of her lightweight sweater; it was already hot, and promising to get hotter.

"It's only June," Fox said, noticing her action. "Wait until August."

"I think I'd rather not," Cindy replied faintly. "I melt in the heat."

"I think it's heredity," Fox observed. "Northern Europeans seem to thrive in a cooler, wetter climate."

This statement made Cindy think of his mother. "You're obviously very fond of your father's people," she said carefully. "Don't you identify at all with your mother?"

"Why should I?" he answered simply. "She didn't identify with me."

"You've never had any contact with her?" Cindy persisted, wondering if she might be pushing him too far, but eager to understand everything about him.

He was silent for a few moments, considering her question, or his answer to it. Then he said, "When she left me with my father, she said she didn't want to be bothered about me in the future. 'Bothered' was the exact word. I gather that I was an embarrassment, not exactly the right bloodline, you understand. As a small child I was curious, of course, but once I became old enough to understand the implications of the situation, I realized that contacting her would be futile, and probably painful. I don't want anybody who doesn't want me," he concluded in a defiant tone that brought quick tears to Cindy's eyes. In those words she heard the child's rejection, and the man's determined vow to overcome it.

"It was her loss, Drew," she said to him, with a catch in her voice that she hoped he missed.

He didn't miss it. He glanced at her and smiled briefly. "Don't be unhappy, princess. It was a long time ago."

"I can't imagine a mother abandoning her child that way," Cindy added slowly.

"No, I'm sure you can't," he replied, in a tone which made her turn her head to look at him.

"Don't hate her, Drew," Cindy said. "She was weak, and you're not. It's always difficult to understand a flaw in someone's character when you don't share it."

"I don't hate her, anymore. When I was younger, her leaving me was sad, but now it's only...interesting."

"Interesting?" What an odd choice of words.

"Yes. I felt sorry for my father, when he was alive, because he loved her. He carried that sorrow to his grave. But now that he's gone, so is the reason for the emptiness she left. I never knew her, and so I never missed her."

"What was he like?"

Fox glanced at her. "My father?"

"Yes."

A small smile played about his lips. "Quiet. Very smart, but not showy about it. He loved me, and I miss that. In anyone's life, there are only a few people, if that, who love that way—completely, selflessly. He was that person for me, and I know I'll never be loved like that again."

Cindy was silent, unable to get words past the lump in her throat. *This* was the man Paula saw as aloof and uninvolved? She didn't know him. She simply didn't know him.

Her reverie was interrupted by a chuckle from Fox, low and self-conscious. "Wow. You sure are getting me to talk. I don't think I've blabbed that much about myself in twenty years. The FBI could use your services."

"I didn't mean to pry," Cindy said, surreptitiously dabbing her damp lashes with a fingertip.

"You didn't. Something about you gets me going. In more ways than one," he concluded dryly, and she could feel her face growing warm.

He glanced over his shoulder and pulled off the road into a grove of orange trees. A fruit stand stood at the edge of the orchard.

"Would you like a drink?" he asked. "It's great stuff, fresh squeezed, the best in the state."

"Oh, yes, please. I'm getting awfully thirsty in this heat."

Fox helped her out of the truck and she sat at an oak table under the trees while he went to get the drinks. He returned with two tall wax cups filled with orange juice swimming with pulp. He handed her one and watched with amusement as she swallowed half the contents in one gulp.

"Fabulous," she pronounced, pausing to take a breath. "Delicious."

He shook his head as he drank from his own glass. "It doesn't take much to please you, does it?" he asked rhetorically.

"Cold juice on a hot day would please anybody," she answered.

"That's not what I meant," he said, but when she looked at him inquiringly, he merely shook his head again and didn't elaborate.

Cindy watched him as he stood a few feet away from her, one leg up on the bench where she sat, an elbow propped on his upraised knee. His shirt was open at the neck, exposing the strong column of his throat. The honey-tan skin glowed with the dull finish of polished marble warmed by the sun. His eyes, narrowed against the glare of the sun, were emerald slits outlined by black lashes as thick as a child's. A slight breeze ruffled his hair and scattered the wisps, like drifting black feathers, across his forehead.

"Why do you look at me like that?" he asked abruptly, and Cindy started, chagrined that she was caught staring.

"I . . ." she said and stopped.

"You what?" he prompted. "You can tell me."

"I like to look at you," she answered simply.

His expression changed, became intent, listening. "Why?"

"Your features are different, intriguing, a combination of traits that shouldn't go together but somehow do. You don't look like anybody else."

"That makes me sound like a freak," he said, half smiling, half serious.

"Oh, no," she protested, concerned that he had misunderstood her. "I think you're beautiful."

He tossed away his empty cup and reached her in two strides, pulling her into his arms.

"You keep saying things like that to me," he whispered against her hair, "and we'll never make it to Eli's."

"Who's Eli?" Cindy asked dreamily, her eyes closing.

"My grandfather," Fox replied, a trace of amusement in his voice. "Remember him?"

"Vaguely," she sighed, relaxing into his shoulder, and he laughed softly.

"Miss Warren, you wouldn't be making a pass at me in a public place, would you? What an unprincesslike thing to do."

Cindy pulled back to look into his eyes, making sure that he was kidding. He grinned wickedly and then kissed the tip of her nose.

"You'd never forget yourself so far, would you, princess? Well, you're not exactly what I'm used to, but a refreshing change." He hugged her briefly and then set her away from him, wagging his finger under her nose. "Now you must promise to behave yourself and not make any more disarming statements."

Cindy's brow knit in puzzlement. "I don't know what you mean, Drew. You asked me a question, and I answered it honestly. You wouldn't want me to lie, would you?"

Fox studied her for a moment, and then asked quietly, "Do you have a boyfriend back home in Pennsylvania—somebody special?"

"No, not really."

"Nobody?"

"Well, I've dated a few other graduate students casually, but that's not what you're talking about, right?"

"How about before, in college, or in high school?"

Cindy considered the question. "Well, I went to an all-girls' school until I was eighteen, and then in college I was usually pretty busy, trying to keep my scholarship. It was a work scholarship, and I had to hold down a campus job and keep my grades up and..."

She stopped talking when she saw that he was waving his hand in a gesture of dismissal. "So you're saying that you've never had a serious relationship with a man?"

"No, I never have."

His expression indicated that he found the information incredible. "What's wrong with the men up north?" he asked, as if talking to himself. "Are they blind, or dead?"

Cindy shifted uncomfortably, sensing that this new awareness on his part might change their relationship.

He glanced at his watch and extended his hand. "We'd better get going, princess. Eli gets itchy if anybody's late; he still doesn't trust cars, considers horses an infinitely more reliable form of transportation."

They climbed back into the truck to complete the journey, but Cindy could tell that he hadn't forgotten what she told him in the grove. He was quiet and thoughtful for the rest of the drive, and she began to wonder if she'd been wrong to tell him the truth. Maybe she should have pretended to experience she didn't have. But as soon as that idea formed in her mind, she dismissed it. He would have been able to tell, he seemed able to read her easily. Still, his reaction worried her. If he preferred sophisticated women who'd been around with a lot of men, she wouldn't interest him.

After about twenty minutes more on the main road Fox turned off onto a dirt track that wound through citrus groves and scrub grass for another couple of miles. At its end the vegetation became denser, until the path stopped in an area fronting a still lake. In the background, right on the shore, stood a stucco house with a large rear veranda completely enclosed by screens.

Fox had barely turned off the motor when the front door of the house opened and a young man in his twenties came out, wearing a straw Stetson with the inevitable jeans and work boots. His shirt was different, however; definitely handmade, with the distinctive Seminole multicolored stripes. Fox was helping Cindy out of the truck as he greeted them.

"Hey, Drew, good to see you." He eyed Cindy appreciatively. "Who is this?"

"Cindy, this is my cousin, Walter Fox. Walter, this is Cindy Warren, from Pennsylvania," Fox said.

"Pennsylvania," Walter echoed, extending his hand. "That's somewhere up around the north pole, isn't it?"

Cindy shook hands with Walter, smiling. "You've got the general direction right, though not quite so far."

"Walter thinks civilization stops at the Florida border," Fox said. He glanced at the house. "Is the old man inside?" he asked Walter.

As if in answer to a summons, the screen door to the patio opened and a man emerged. Cindy watched his approach, hoping that Eli would like her.

If she had had some idea of Fox's grandfather as a bent, shriveled ancient in a serape, smoking a corn cob pipe, it was quickly dispelled when she met him.

"Cindy, this is my grandfather, Eli Fox," her companion said. "Eli, this is Cindy Warren, the friend I told you about."

Cindy's hand was lost in the old man's weathered one as she wondered what Fox had said. Eli looked her over, his keen eyes missing nothing. He was robust, with streaks of white running through his coal-black hair, and looked much younger than his years. He was shorter and more Indian in appearance than Drew.

Dressed in tan shorts and a polo shirt, with thongs on his bare feet, he looked like a Long Island retiree about to water his zinnias.

"How do you do?" he said politely. "Andrew tells me that you are interested in our legends and would like to talk to me about them."

"Yes, if you have the time. I'm doing a paper on the folklore of the southeastern Indians."

"A college paper?" he asked, faint amusement showing in his tone.

"Yes, a master's thesis."

"Do you hear that, Andrew? They're teaching college courses on our spirit stories now."

"Yeah, Eli, I know," Fox replied, smiling indulgently at Cindy. "Do you think you can help this young lady with her research while Walter and I do the lawn?"

"Certainly," Eli said, making a sweeping gesture toward his back porch. "Will you join me on the patio? The boys get together to do the yard work about once a month. I tell them I can handle it, but they think I'm a feeble shut-in incapable of manual labor."

This was so far from the obvious truth that Cindy laughed. "Oh, Mr. Fox, I don't think anyone would make that mistake about you," she said, as they walked together to the veranda. It was pleasant and cool inside, and a pitcher of iced tea had already been prepared. It was on a stand just beside the door. Cindy could hear the voices of Drew and his cousin as they assembled their tools, and soon the soothing drone of the mower punctuated the late morning stillness.

"Call me Eli," Fox's grandfather said, as they sat down on the lawn chairs provided, and he poured the tea. "Now," he went on, handing her a glass and settling back in his chair, "how did you meet my grandson?"

Cindy described the rather unorthodox circumstances of their meeting to the old man, who nodded and seemed to find nothing strange about his grandson diving through a window onto Council Rock's main street. In his turn he told her about his move to this new house, how Fox persuaded him that he would be better off in modern surroundings, and how Fox took great pains to find property where his grandfather would be comfortable. His every word was suffused with love for his dead son's child, and Cindy found herself thinking that while Fox might have lacked a mother's care, he had missed nothing of affection thanks to these people who had raised him.

"Well, enough of this," Eli said suddenly, interrupting himself. "How can I help you?"

Cindy removed a yellow legal pad from her large purse. "I'd like to ask you some questions, and I'd like to take notes, if I may."

Eli gestured for her to scribble away.

"I'm especially interested in the Green Corn Ceremony, the *busk*, as you call it. Can you describe to me the rituals involved, and the stories that were told?"

Eli nodded and launched into a flood of remembrance that gave Cindy writer's cramp trying to keep up with him. The information was pure gold, however, and she had filled several pages with her own brand of shorthand when a sound from outside caused her to look up.

Fox was cutting the weeds at the side of the driveway with a scythe. Stripped to the waist, his muscular torso streaming sweat, he swung the tool in a rhythmic arc, his whole body swaying gracefully in time to the motion of his arms. Cindy stared for several seconds before tearing her eyes away, but Eli had noticed her attention wandering from their interview.

"My grandson is attractive," he observed quietly, glancing from the girl before him to the driveway and then back again.

Though somewhat startled, Cindy answered frankly. "Yes."

"He is very appealing to you, very sexual," the old man continued, watching her reaction.

Cindy could feel the flush climbing into her skin, but she answered again, "Yes."

Eli nodded. "It was the same with my son and Andrew's mother. The heat between them was obvious, you could see it, almost touch it."

Her face flaming, unable to believe that she was having this conversation with Drew's *grandfather*, Cindy said quietly, "Mr. Fox, if you are making comparisons between Drew's mother and me, saying that I am like her..."

Eli shook his head once, decisively. "You are not like her, and my name is Eli."

Cindy smiled, relaxing. "I'm glad to hear you say that."

"What, that my name is Eli?" he asked, twinkling, and she laughed.

"You have a nice laugh," he observed. "No, you are nothing like her. She was earthy, aggressive, outgoing—she chased my son. Now, I would say that in your case Andrew is doing the chasing."

"But I'm not running away," Cindy said, meeting his wise black eyes.

Eli sighed. "You must understand my concern. When I see *another* of the Fox men bringing home *another* beautiful *shankree* girl, I worry."

"I'm not beautiful," Cindy began.

"Of course you are." He made a dismissive gesture, as if the subject merited no further discussion. "And Andrew likes you. He likes you very much."

"How can you tell?" Cindy asked, her curiosity overruling her manners.

"You're here," Eli answered. "You're the first friend he has ever brought to meet me."

Cindy was silent, taking that in.

"You seem confused," Eli said. "Don't you know what it is that he likes?"

Cindy raised her eyes to his, waiting.

"You have a sweetness, an innocence that even I can see. You're different to him, the lady in the tower in one of those Anglo-Saxon fairy tales."

Rapunzel, Cindy thought. Eli was right.

"But that's not me," Cindy protested. "I don't want him to like some ideal, some illusion that doesn't exist."

Eli folded his arms on his chest and examined her closely. "Don't you like to read and to study, as Andrew told me? Don't you like to be alone with your thoughts? Don't you prefer the world of ideas to harsh realities?"

"I guess so," Cindy admitted, not liking to hear herself described in exactly that way.

"Then Andrew is not wrong, is he?" Eli asked.

"I guess not," Cindy replied, and they both laughed.

Fox appeared at the door in time to hear the burst of laughter. "Well, it looks like you two are getting along famously," he commented, shrugging into his shirt. "How's it going, princess? Did you get what you need?"

"More than enough," Cindy replied. "Your grandfather was very helpful."

He nodded. "Well, I'll just wash up inside and then we'll be on our way." He glanced at his grandfather. "Everything's done. Walter is going to finish up the edging when the sun goes down and it's cooler."

"Thank you, Andrew," the old man said, with ineffable dignity. "But can't you stay for lunch? Walter and I can get something together."

"No thanks, Eli. Cindy and I have plans." He winked at Cindy as he walked past her into the house. "Be right back," he added, and vanished.

Cindy's eyes followed him, wondering what the plans were.

"When he leaves the room, the light goes with him, doesn't it?" the old man said, studying her expression.

Cindy nodded, unable to say it any better.

"Come back," Eli invited her. "Come back whenever you like—if you need more information for your paper, or if you just want to visit."

"Thank you," Cindy said. "I'd like to make the trip again, with Drew."

"Oh, who needs him?" Eli said, sniffing. "I hope I don't need my good-looking grandson to attract the attention of a pretty girl." He leaned in closer to her and whispered conspiratorially, "Come without him and I'll show you all his embarrassing baby pictures."

Cindy grinned.

"You like that idea, do you?" Eli said, grinning back. Fox returned to find them smiling at each other.

"I think I'd better get this young lady out of here before you marry her, Eli," he announced dryly and reached for Cindy's hand. She allowed him to pull her to her feet and felt her pulse quicken as he slipped his arm casually around her waist.

"I'll be back on Tuesday," Fox said to his grandfather. "Try not to let the grass grow between now and then."

"I'll do my best," Eli said, raising his hand in farewell. "And remember what I said," he called to Cindy as she smiled goodbye.

"I'll remember," she answered.

"What did he say?" Fox asked, as they waved to Walter, who was riding the mower back into the storage shed.

"That's between your grandfather and me," Cindy answered airily.

"Secrets already," Fox sighed, opening the door of the cab for her.

"By the way, what are our 'plans' for lunch?" Cindy asked.

"Our plans are not to subject ourselves to Walter's horrendous cooking," Fox replied, leaning on the open door and looking in at her. "He specializes in rubber omelets and incinerated hamburgers."

"I see," Cindy said, laughing. "But there's one problem. I'm starving."

Fox spread his hands. "Hey, you're looking at a man who's always prepared." He pointed to the flatbed in back, where she saw a styrofoam hamper through the window. "There's our lunch. Sandwiches, salad, dessert, the works."

"You didn't make all that?" Cindy asked.

"Hell, no. I ordered it from the deli in town and picked it up before I came for you."

"But what about poor Walter and Eli, passing out from hunger back there at the house?" Cindy reproached him, drawing down the corners of her mouth.

Fox favored her with a superior smile. "I got one for them, too, and left it in the kitchen with a note."

Cindy shook her head in feigned amazement. "I give up; you think of everything. But I'd guess that your relatives are going to find it mighty suspicious that we didn't stay to share the picnic with them."

"Who cares what they think?" he answered, slamming the door. "By now they're too deep into the cole slaw to wonder about anything." He went around the back of the truck and got in next to her. "Besides, I want to show you something."

Cindy settled back against the seat as he drove away, content to go where he would lead her.

Five

—

Fox guided the truck further down the dirt road that had brought them to Eli's house. The lake spread away from them to the right, and Cindy caught glimpses of its blue sparkle through the passing rush of the trees. After another mile Fox pulled off the road into a clearing and stopped the truck.

"What's this?" she asked, as he helped her to the ground and then took the styrofoam hamper from the back. He grabbed up a checkered tablecloth that had been folded under it and handed it to Cindy.

"This is my uncle's place," he answered. "It's just a short walk through the cypresses. Stay to the path and follow behind me."

"Are there snakes?" Cindy asked nervously, picking her way gingerly after him and clutching the tablecloth to her chest.

"Water moccasins, I think," he replied casually. "Rattlers too, maybe a few boa constrictors."

Cindy stopped walking until she thought about the last thing he'd said. "Wait a minute," she said suspiciously. "I'm not sure about the first two, but even I know there are no boa constrictors in Florida."

He turned and faced her, his eyebrows raised. "See? All those years in college have not been in vain."

"You're not funny, Fox," she said, and stepped on something which moved. She yelped and jumped backward, dropping both the cloth and her purse.

Wearing an expression of extreme forbearance, Fox set the hamper down and picked her up in the same smooth motion. "That does it, I'm carrying you," he said, and proceeded to do so, threading through the trees expertly.

"What about our stuff?" Cindy asked contentedly, not really caring, her arms around his neck and her head on his shoulder. He smelled of his hours in the sun, as if his skin had been baked to its perfect golden color.

"I'll go back for it, once I'm sure you won't be taking on the wildlife and losing," he answered, turning to sidestep the stump of a gnarled oak. He took the opportunity to spin her in dizzying circles until, laughing, she begged him to stop.

"Had enough?" he asked, lowering her weight suddenly, pretending he was about to drop her. "Say uncle."

"Uncle, uncle," she gasped, clutching his shirt, breathless.

"I don't know," he said, debating. "You don't sound very sincere." He shifted her suddenly, tossing her over his shoulder in a fireman's carry. "That's much better," he announced, as she kicked in protest. "Puts more distance between you and the piranhas."

"Piranhas are *fish*," she squealed, laughing so hard she could hardly get the words out. "Don't you think I know anything? Now put me down and let me walk."

He ignored her, proceeding on course until they broke through the screen of trees and reached the shore.

"What do you think?" he asked, setting her down gently, keeping his arms around her so that she was standing with her back to him, his hands folded across her waist.

"Oh, Drew, it's lovely," she breathed, taking in the placid, sun-spattered surface of the water, the dense circle of encroaching cypresses all along the shore, the cloudless vault of the sky. "Where are we?"

"This is my uncle's place," he answered, his voice in her ear. "I built the *chiksee* just around that bend to the left. He always meant to build a house here, but he never made it."

"Why not?"

"He's in jail," Fox answered calmly. "For twenty years."

Cindy turned within the circle of his embrace to look at him. "Why? What did he do?"

"He killed the man who had raped his wife," Fox replied, watching her reaction to his statement.

"Oh, Drew, how awful," she whispered, trying to comprehend the enormity of it.

"If you were my wife, I'd do the same to anybody who touched you," he said flatly, in a tone that left no doubt that he meant it. Cindy felt a chill which had nothing to do with the weather.

"Don't you think you'd better go back for the basket?" she asked, wanting to change the subject.

"Stay right here," he directed. "Don't wander off."

She nodded. She barely heard his footsteps through the trees; he was very quiet in his movements for a big man. When he returned she was rooted to the same spot, waiting.

"Here's the grub," he said, spreading the cloth on the ground and setting out the wrapped packages and plastic containers. When it was all displayed they both looked at it.

"I guess I've lost my appetite," Cindy said, and turned away.

He was beside her in a second. "Did I scare you, princess?" he asked, taking hold of her shoulders and forcing her to look at him.

"A little," she admitted. "I don't like to hear you talk that way."

He enfolded her slowly, sighing deeply. "I'm sorry. It's just that, since I met you, I can understand how my uncle must have felt. When I think of somebody putting his hands on you, treating you roughly, forcing you...." The sentence trailed off as his hands tightened on her arms.

"Shhh," Cindy said, silencing him. "We shouldn't have come here; I didn't know about your uncle. It must be terrible for you to be reminded of all that."

"Not as terrible as it is for him to live it. I visit him with Walter. You should see my uncle now. He used to be so strong, so capable. Now he's a beaten man."

"What became of his wife?" Cindy asked.

"She died a few years after he went to jail," Fox replied. "I was about twenty-five, I guess. Some disease, they said it was, but I think the whole tragedy just slowly killed her." He held her off and looked at her. "Come on, princess, eat something. You don't want to leave this feast for the squirrels."

They sat together on the ground, and once Cindy tasted some of the food, her appetite returned. Everything was very good, and Fox produced tumblers of ice-cold water from a well on the property that still worked. When they had packed away the leftovers he reclined on the tablecloth, using it as a blanket, and gestured for her to join him. When Cindy sat at his side, he pulled her down with him, molding her to his body. She relaxed against his shoulder, resting her cheek on his chest.

"So what do you think of my kingdom?" Fox asked, gesturing with his free hand.

"Is that what this is?" Cindy asked, looking around at the blue expanse of lake and sky.

"Certainly. And you're the captive princess from a foreign northern land who has been whisked away to dwell with me in the underworld."

Cindy smiled, closing her eyes and inhaling the clean fragrance of his skin, his soap. "I think you've got a few stories all mixed up there, Mr. Fox."

He changed position so that she was lying flat on her back and he was looking down at her. "But I'm perfectly clear on one thing," he said.

"What's that?" Cindy asked, gazing up into the green eyes which seemed to fill the world.

"The way I feel about you," he answered, and kissed her.

His mouth was so warm and soft, its pressure on hers so leisurely, that Cindy's lips opened almost without volition. He kissed her for a long time, barely touching her except with his mouth, until she reached behind his head and pulled him closer, unconsciously inviting more. He reacted instantly, enfolding her, pressing her into the curve of his body, and his mouth slipped from hers to the hollow of her throat.

"You're driving me crazy," he murmured. "I've been trying to hold back with you, but I don't think I can do it anymore."

Cindy moved, and he groaned, burying his flushed face in her neck. He lowered his weight onto her, holding himself up on his hands until their bodies were fused and then relaxing gradually. Cindy instinctively shifted to accommodate him, and then gasped as she felt the hardness of his desire, the muscular tension in his strong arms and lean, racehorse legs. His mouth sought hers again, and this time he abandoned all attempts to go slow. His tongue caressed hers as his hands came up to the buttons at the front of her sweater. Lost in his

kisses, Cindy couldn't object as he unbuttoned them
and slipped his fingers inside the opening. His hand was
hot, and yet gentle, cupping her breast through the lace
brassiere and teasing the taut nipple with his thumb.
Cindy moaned, turning her face away from his, lost in
the sensation. He lowered his head, running his parted
lips over the smooth skin he had exposed to view. His
hands moved down to her hips, grasping them and
forcing them upward into his. With one hand he lifted
her skirt and sought the silken smoothness of her thighs,
pressing her legs outward to allow him to lie more fully
between them. The barrier of their clothing seemed to
evaporate as Cindy knew, for the first time, what it
must be like to receive a man.

"Do you want me?" he rasped, reaching for the zip-
per on her skirt. "Do you want me to take you
now?"

Hearing him say it caused the flood tide of passion to
recede long enough for reason to reassert itself. Cindy
stiffened, and he felt it immediately. He sat up and
gazed at her silently, his eyes glittering like gemstones.

"I can't do this, Drew," she said, putting the back of
her hand to her mouth. "I want you, surely you can tell
that, but this just isn't right."

"Why?" he said angrily. "Is it beneath your high-
ness to grovel in the grass with a savage like me?"

"Cheap shot, Drew," she said sharply, her mouth
tightening. "That isn't true and you know it."

"I'm sorry," he said in a low tone, looking away.
"You don't deserve a remark like that."

Cindy rose to her feet, straightening her clothes. "I'm going for a walk," she said shakily, seizing on the first idea that came into her head.

His fists clenched at his sides. "Don't run away from me," he said, agonized. "Please."

"I'm not running away from you," she replied, and it was the truth. She was running away from herself.

"You'll get lost," he said, moving to get up also.

"Don't," Cindy said quickly. "Don't follow me, Drew; I need some time alone. I'll keep to the shoreline and I won't go far, all right?"

Fox subsided reluctantly, sitting back on his haunches, his expression grave as he watched her walk away.

Cindy wandered along the edge of the water, her sandals sinking into the marshy grass. She took them off and carried them, walking barefoot, her mind a jumble of confusing images and thoughts.

She didn't know what to do. If she continued to see Fox, sooner or later their mutual passion would burst out of control, but the thought of not seeing him any more was unbearable. She'd never felt like this before, and her experience with men was so limited that she was unable to determine how to handle the situation. She couldn't become just another one of Fox's lovers, but she couldn't give him up either. With him, she was alive in a way that was new to her. Up until the time she met him, her books and studies and quiet life had been sufficient. She hadn't known what she was missing, like a person born blind who can't appreciate the glory of a sun he has never seen. But now—she couldn't go back to that former existence now. It would never again be enough.

Cindy pressed her fingers to her temples, trying to think. At the same time she caught sight of a structure in the distance, partially hidden by the trees. Curious, she moved forward, rounding a bend in the shoreline and confronting a little house made of logs and leaves. The *chiksee*, she thought. This was Fox's construction, abandoned but still sturdy, silent and waiting, like a summer cottage restless for the return of its warm-weather occupants.

Cindy studied the *chiksee*, thinking about the care that had gone into the placement of every strip of bark, every leaf, and her throat tightened. What sort of man would build this from scratch, taking the time to put it together as his ancestors once had, just to see if he could do it? Others saw the tough exterior, the bounty hunter who chased human quarry for a living. But he had wanted Cindy to see another side of him, the man who loved his family and this isolated spot on a lonely lake.

Taking a deep, quavering breath, Cindy came to a decision. She was going to stick with this, take it one step at a time, and hope she could deal with it. Fox was too special for her to do anything else. If she turned away from him, she would be sorry for the rest of her life.

Walking slowly, she retraced her steps to the clearing where Fox awaited her. As she came closer she saw that he was lying on the tablecloth, and then she realized from his loose, boneless posture that he was asleep.

Tiptoeing, she approached stealthily until she was standing over him, gazing down at his slumbering form.

I'll bet he got almost no sleep last night, she thought, remembering his remark about napping in the truck. There were blue shadows of fatigue under his eyes, and his body was sprawled in the careless, abandoned manner of pure exhaustion.

Cindy glanced at her watch. She hated to wake him, but she had promised Paula that she would be back by five to monitor the phone. The woman who shared management duties with Paula was sick, and Paula had to work a double shift at the hospital in order to get a three-day weekend she'd requested.

Cindy sat next to him, tucking her legs under her and touching his shoulder. He stirred slightly, turning toward her, and his shirt, loosened by her eager hands earlier, rode up on his midriff.

Cindy sucked in her breath. His ribs were taped all along his left side, and a deep, angry scratch below them was painted vivid carmine with iodine.

She bit her lower lip, her eyes moving to his placid face. He must have been in pain all day with this, and yet he had given no sign, even doing the lawn work at his grandfather's house. She and Eli had seen him only from the back, and nothing in his movements had indicated the presence of such an injury.

Cindy tugged at his arm, harder, until the thick lashes lifted and he looked into her eyes. He was alert immediately, sitting up and looking around him.

"It's all right," Cindy assured him. "You were only sleeping about half an hour."

He nodded and stretched, showing the white markings of the tape once again.

"Drew, how did you get that?" Cindy asked quietly, pointing.

He glanced down at himself, and then at her. "I'll have to be a little neater in the future," he said dryly, tucking in his shirt.

"You didn't answer my question."

Fox shrugged. "The guy I went after last week didn't agree that it was time for him to return to jail. He gave me some trouble, that's all."

"That's all!" she echoed, incredulous. "Drew, you should have told me that you were hurt. You shouldn't be out with me today; you should be in bed, resting."

"Cindy, if I went to bed every time something like this happened on the job, I'd spend most of my time flat on my back." He got to his feet, looking around for their scattered things.

"Is that all you can say?" Cindy challenged him.

He met her eyes. "No, that's not all. I thought the time with you today was too important to miss, and that's why I said nothing about my... mishap. I figured you'd react just like this."

Cindy dropped her eyes. She was only beginning to realize how dangerous his lifestyle was.

"Does this sort of thing happen often?" she asked in a small voice.

"Now and then," he said vaguely, picking up the hamper and setting it aside, shaking out the tablecloth. She bent to help him, and he caught her hand.

"Cindy, I want to ask you something."

She waited.

"About what happened before, you don't think I brought you here to...seduce you, do you?"

She met his gaze squarely. "No, Drew, I never thought that."

His relief was only partial. "I just wanted you to see my special place, that's all. I know that it's secluded, but I honestly wasn't thinking about getting you alone or anything."

His insistence was almost ingenuous, and she smiled. "Forget it, Drew. Now can we get this show on the road before the ants eat my ankles?"

He nodded, unsmiling, and they packed up to go.

Fox was silent on the way back to the truck, and Cindy wondered what he was thinking. There were no cute remarks about the wildlife underfoot or killer fish. Cindy missed the teasing banter, but his demeanor was serious and it didn't look like it was going to change. When he handed her into the truck she smiled at him, and he didn't smile back.

The drive home seemed to pass in a blur of sun-struck palms and roadside stands. By the time they reached Paula's apartment Cindy was convinced he was going to tell her that they shouldn't see each other again. And why not? Other women didn't refuse him; they didn't make him work so hard. Cindy had heard enough from Paula to understand that, but she also knew that she couldn't change her personality to suit his expectations. She was sitting in wordless misery, her hands folded in her lap like a gradeschooler about to get a scolding, when Fox pulled into a parking place and shut off the motor.

"I'll take you up," he said briefly, and walked at her side up the two sets of stairs, a trip that took an eternity. When they came to a halt outside Paula's door, Cindy took a deep breath and looked into his eyes.

"Thank you for my lovely day, Drew," she said, making a brave attempt to finish everything gracefully.

He stared at her for a second, and then, with a sound like a broken sigh, he cupped her face in his hands.

"What a well brought-up young lady you are," he said quietly, rubbing his thumbs gently over her lower lip. "You look like you're about to cry, and yet you're able to say the right thing. Come on, princess, the last part of it wasn't so lovely."

"It was *too* lovely, Drew. That was the problem."

He closed his eyes, and it was several seconds before he replied. "Cindy, your honesty is going to get both of us into trouble," he said huskily, closing her lips with his fingers. "Don't you know women aren't supposed to make admissions like that?"

"Why not, if it's the truth." She turned her head, avoiding his touch. "I didn't want you to think that what happened was your fault."

He grasped her chin between his thumb and forefinger, forcing her to look at him. "You're not mad at me, then?" he asked, searching her face.

"No, of course not. Did you think I was?"

He dropped his eyes. "I wasn't sure. You're always so polite. I thought maybe you were just toughing it out

Escape with 4 FREE Silhouette Desire Novels (a $9.00 value) and get a Mystery Gift, too!

until you got home." He shrugged. "Even if you did think the worst of me I figured you'd never tell me."

"But what about my famous honesty?" she asked, and he shook his head.

"It would take a backseat to sparing my feelings, though, wouldn't it?" he answered, and she permitted herself a slight nod.

"Thought so." He placed his hands on her shoulders. "Now, with that behind us, can we start over?"

"By all means."

He grinned, his first real smile since she woke him up at the beach. "Okay. I have to go down to the DA's office to give a deposition, but it should only take an hour or so. Why don't you change clothes, and I'll pick you up later. We can go someplace nice for dinner."

"Drew, I can't. I promised Paula I would stay here tonight and monitor the phone."

He looked annoyed. "Doesn't she have an answering machine?"

Cindy shook her head. "That's not the point. She's an assistant manager of the complex, and she's paid to have a real person on duty to respond to real emergencies."

"Then why isn't *she* doing it?"

"She has to work. Come on, Drew, I'm doing her a favor. You can understand that."

His expression grudging, he said, "I guess so." He smiled dryly. "You can see that I don't like anything to interfere with my plans." He brightened. "I know. I'll get some take-out stuff and bring it back here for us."

Cindy didn't reply.

He read her silence correctly. "No good, huh?" He eyed her intently. "Afraid to be alone with me?"

"No, Drew, that's not it. It's Paula's place and I don't think it would be right for me to have company here when she's not home."

Fox rolled his eyes. "You take this Miss Manners thing too seriously, do you know that?"

She was about to protest when he raised his hand, forestalling her. "All right, all right. Far be it for me to question your judgment on etiquette, though I think Paula is the last person on earth who would care."

"I'd care," Cindy said, and he relented.

"I'll call you later, okay?" he said softly, stroking her hair.

"Okay," she said, and then touched his arm. He studied her, waiting for the question he could sense was coming.

"Drew, why do you have to give a deposition on a Saturday night? Is it an emergency or something?"

He looked as though he regretted bringing it up. "Sort of," he hedged.

"What does that mean?"

He sighed heavily, his shoulders slumping. It was a gesture of resignation, and she knew that he was about to tell her.

"You know that guy who gave me this?" he said, pointing to his taped ribs.

She nodded mutely.

"Well, I tracked him down in a bar, and when I tried to pick him up he created kind of a ruckus. He came at me with a broken beer bottle, but somebody got in the way and took the cut instead. I have to give my version of what happened and swear to it."

Cindy licked her lips, which were suddenly dry. "Drew, that could have been you. He meant to hurt you."

"It wasn't," he said firmly. "It wasn't me, and I don't want you to think about it anymore."

"I'm not sure I'll be able to follow those orders," she replied, looking away from him.

The phone rang inside the apartment, and Cindy quickly unlocked the door. "I have to get that," she said, glancing back at Fox.

He leaned forward and kissed her briefly on the forehead. "Go ahead," he answered. "I'll call you later," he repeated.

She left the door ajar, and she heard him whistling as he walked away.

He didn't call. All that evening, every time the phone rang, Cindy was sure it was Fox. But she heard from three tenants, Paula's aunt, and her own mother, everyone but the person she most wanted to be on the other end of the line. As it got later, she began to worry. What could have happened to him? She knew that he would have kept his word if it were possible, and the only conclusion she could come to was that something was wrong.

Paula returned from the hospital around eleven-thirty, so exhausted from her double shift that she didn't pause for conversation but just stumbled into bed. Cindy fretted for another hour and a half, and then

went to bed, certain that she would not be able to sleep.
She had pulled the phone, with its long extension cord,
into her room, and she drifted in and out of a fitful
doze, waiting for it to ring.

When it finally did, she jumped up so suddenly that
she knocked over the lamp on her bedside table, while
reaching for the receiver. She winced as it crashed into
the wall, and then plunged to the floor, making enough
noise to wake Paula, and possibly several of her de-
ceased relatives.

After scrabbling for the receiver in the dark, Cindy
lifted it to her mouth and said, "Drew?"

"Yeah, it's me." He sounded very tired.

"Drew, what happened? Where are you? Are you all
right?"

"I'm fine. I'm at the county jail."

Her heart missed a beat. "You haven't been ar-
rested?"

"No, no. Although it would hardly surprise anyone
if I had been." He paused, and she heard a deep inhal-
ation. He was smoking.

"I got held up after I gave the deposition," he explained. "The assistant DA who took it brought me
over here to look at a lineup. A jumper I caught a few
years ago got out on parole and killed a woman. He was
using an assumed name, and I had to identify him as the
person I returned to custody, and the victim's daughter
had to identify him as the guy she saw leaving her
mother's house." He didn't say the experience had been
harrowing, but she could hear it in his drained, tone-
less delivery.

"Killed," Cindy repeated. "He killed a woman?"

"That's what the prosecutor thinks," Fox replied. "And from what I know of the guy, I certainly wouldn't put it past him."

There was a brief knock, and then Cindy's door opened. Paula entered the room, wearing two ounces of lace lingerie and a pained expression.

"What broke?" she demanded. "I heard a noise."

"Just a second," Cindy said into the phone, and then covered the mouthpiece.

"The lamp fell," Cindy replied to Paula, "but it didn't break. I'm sorry. I knocked it over in the dark."

Paula, her shadowy form outlined by the hall light behind her, folded her arms. "Who's that on the phone? As if I didn't know."

"It's Drew," Cindy answered patiently.

"Somebody ought to buy that guy a watch," Paula stated irritably and slammed Cindy's door behind her.

"I guess Paula heard the phone," Fox said when she got back on the line.

"Yes," Cindy said, not going into the rest of it.

"Look, I'm sorry I woke both of you up. I just got involved and the time sped by. It wasn't until later that I realized you might be worried when you didn't hear from me."

"I was worried. I couldn't sleep."

"It was only a phone call, Cindy. It wasn't like we had a date firmed up and I missed it."

Cindy was silent. Was he chastising her, asserting his independence?

"You still there?" he asked, his tone lighter.

"I'm still here."

"All right," he said. "I'm a jerk. I'm not used to anybody worrying about me, that's all. I really was tied up with the police until a few minutes ago. I would have waited until morning to get in touch, but I'll be gone by then."

"Gone?" she repeated faintly, her spirits sinking further.

"Yeah, I have to drive up to Alabama for an extradition hearing. The state police just located the guy and it's set for first thing Monday morning. I can't get a flight in time so I have to take my car. The town is a long distance from the nearest airport and it's actually faster to drive."

"Drew, you can't drive. You've had no sleep for two nights running," she said, distracted by visions of him gliding onto off ramps and into telephone poles.

"Cindy, I have to get there. Unless this creep is extradited to Georgia he'll get away with defrauding a bunch of old people in his nursing homes of all their retirement funds. He fled jurisdiction when the feds caught on to him, and I want to make sure he is punished for it."

Cindy took a breath. "Drew, is your life always like this?" she asked him.

"Pretty much," he answered. "I'm not exactly what you'd call reliable." He paused. "But I guess you've gathered that."

"When will you be back?"

"I don't know. It could be over fast, with just the hearing, or it could take several days."

She didn't know how to handle it. How could she press him for information he didn't have?

"Cindy," he said, "you'll hear from me. I don't know when, but you will."

"Okay, Drew." What else could she say?

"Cindy?"

"Hmm?"

"It's nice that you care what happens to me. I like that." A smile came into his voice. "Look for me . . ."

"Yes, I know. When the sun goes down."

"That's my girl."

"Drew, be careful. Take care of yourself."

"I will. Goodbye, princess."

"Goodbye."

Cindy hung up, falling back on the pillows. She glanced at the lamp which lay in a heap, its shade askew, on the rug. Automatically, she got out of bed and righted it, standing it back on the table.

Could she take this? Could she take Fox's life-style, the pattern of leaving at a moment's notice with no set time of return? He was going off into danger every time he left, and no amount of rationalizing could dismiss that fact.

Cindy shook her head and climbed back into bed. It appeared that she was going to find out if she could live with his precarious adventures.

Because whether she liked it or not, she was falling in love with Andrew Fox.

Six

Five days later Cindy was seated on the floor of Paula's living room with a stack of index cards. She was methodically sorting the cards and then clipping them to the typed pages they outlined. A casual observer witnessing her apparent concentration would not have guessed her inner turmoil.

Paula entered the room and displayed her hand like a model on television selling dishwashing lotion.

"How do you like it?" she asked. "Mango frappe."

Cindy glanced at the iridescent orange nail polish and nodded. "It's very...shiny."

"Not to mention seductive, long wearing, and non-chip," Paula added dryly, quoting from the sales copy.

She watched Cindy bite the cap of her pen, holding it between her teeth and nibbling at it like a ferret.

"Is that what you do instead of smoking?" she asked.

Cindy looked at her uncomprehendingly. "What?"

"Never mind. I take it you haven't heard from him."

Cindy shook her head.

"You have nothing to add?" Paula probed.

Cindy shrugged. "What is there to say? I have no claim on him; he doesn't have to report to me daily as if I were his mother. He said I would hear from him, and I will. Eventually."

"How very mature," Paula said. "And how understanding. Everyone knows there are no phones in Georgia. Or post offices or Western Union operators."

Cindy threw her a dirty look.

"I know, I know," Paula said, holding up her hand. "But, if you ask me, he's using this trip to put emotional distance between you."

"Nobody asked you," Cindy pointed out.

"Has that ever stopped me before?" Paula asked rhetorically.

Cindy sighed and uncoiled her legs, stretching them. "Paula, look at it logically. As of this moment, I have been out with him twice, only once on an actual date. Why should he feel compelled to keep me posted on his every move? I believe that he'll call me when he gets back, and that's sufficient."

Paula nodded patiently. "All that *sounds* wonderful, but I happen to know that you haven't eaten a square meal since he left. You may be convincing your-

self with your splendid reasoning, but I'm not buying
it."

"Then don't," Cindy said shortly, getting up. "Go
back into your bedroom and frappe your toenails."

"Oh, oh," Paula said. "Getting a little miffed, are
we?"

Cindy put her hands on her hips and stared her down.
"I'm getting a little miffed, yes. Your attitude toward
Fox changes with the light. One minute you're wishing
me luck and urging me onward, and the next you're
making wisecracks about his disappearing act. What's
going on, Paula? Are you *trying* to drive me crazy?"

Paula thought that over. "Okay, you're right. I am
vacillating about this whole thing. Sometimes, when I
see how happy you are with him, I want it to work out
and I encourage you. Then, other times, I remember
what he used to be like...." She left the sentence unfinished, for Cindy to draw her own conclusions.

"People can change," Cindy said. "They grow up
and different things become important to them."

"Possibly," Paula said, her tone unconvinced.

"Definitely," Cindy confirmed. "Now go back to
your manicure and let me get this work done." She sat
back down and started shuffling papers.

"I guess I know when I'm not wanted." Paula sniffed
and marched out of the room.

Cindy looked up after she'd gone, and her expression was thoughtful.

The next afternoon, Cindy was sitting at a table in the
back of the reference room when a long shadow fell

across the page she was reading. She glanced up and Fox was towering over her, his expression wary, as if he were unsure of the reception he was going to get.

"Hi," he said. "I'm back."

Cindy smiled. "Hello, Drew. I'm glad to see you."

"Yeah?" he said, tilting his head to one side and looking at her askance.

"Of course. How did the trip go?"

He pulled out a chair and turned it around, seat forward. Lifting one leg over the back of it, he dropped into it.

"Fine," he replied, folding his arms across the top of the ladder-back. "We put that guy away where he'll never cheat anybody again."

"That's good," she said, closing her book carefully. She couldn't help comparing this return with his previous one, when he'd opened his arms and she had run into them. But that was before the lake, before they both realized how much was at stake.

He glanced around at the floor-to-ceiling stacks nervously, as if viewing a lineup of his enemies. "Looks like you've got a few books here," he said, raising his eyebrows. Cindy thought he looked out of place in this arena of higher learning—his tough, lean exterior bespeaking knowledge of a very different kind.

"A few," she replied, making a note in the margin of her pad and putting her pen away. "I like to work here, where I have all the information I need at my fingertips."

"How's the paper coming?" he asked.

"Fine. Right on schedule."

He fell silent and studied her face, while she looked back at him. He was wearing a gray T-shirt with the sleeves cut off, exposing his muscular arms. His jeans and moccasins might have passed for student wear, but despite his clothing he looked about as much like a student as she looked like a fan dancer. He wore his aura of danger like an ornament, and like an ornament, it drew attention. Out of the corner of her eye Cindy saw a couple of girls at the next table staring at him and conversing in hushed whispers. She could guess the subject of their conversation without trying very hard.

"I wasn't going to come here," he said suddenly.

"What do you mean?"

"When I called the apartment Paula told me you were here, but I was going to wait until you got home." He shifted restlessly in his chair. "These places make me jumpy."

"Why?"

He shrugged. "Schools, churches, libraries. I was always getting thrown out of them."

The reference librarian chose that moment to advance on them and glare at Fox.

"You'll have to keep your voices down or go outside," she said sternly. "People are trying to work here."

"See what I mean?" Fox asked Cindy as the woman walked away. "They see me and freak. You'd think I was going to set fire to the joint." He stood, shoving his chair back into place with a loud scraping noise and staring defiantly at the librarian when she looked up.

"Let's get out of here," he concluded, picking up her book pack and shouldering it.

Cindy gathered the rest of her things and followed him down the narrow aisle, then out through the double doors to the hall. Once out of the room Fox expelled a breath, as if he'd been under some tension that had just been released.

"The last time I was in a library was ten years ago," he said, glancing at her. "I was looking up some deeds for my uncle." He smiled and tugged on a strand of her hair. "What were you doing ten years ago?"

"Oh, I don't know. Studying geometry, probably. Or algebra. Math was never my strong point. What were you doing besides looking up deeds?"

He thought about it for a second. "Raising hell, I guess. Making a fool of myself. That was my usual occupation in those days." He pushed open the outer door and they stepped into a flood of sunshine. "Have you got Paula's car?"

Cindy nodded. "It's in the row next to the concrete abutment," she said, pointing.

"I have to go back to my place and check the mail. I'm expecting some legal papers that can't wait." He eyed her speculatively. "Do you want to come along?"

"To your house?"

"Yes."

Cindy hesitated.

"You'll be safe with me," he said quietly.

"I know that," she replied, making her decision. "Should I leave Paula's car here?"

Fox shook his head. "Better follow me. The car will be okay in the lot at my building."

Cindy did as he said, trailing him out of the university lot and following his sports car along the boulevard lined with palm trees that ran parallel to the school. He drove for about two miles and then pulled into a condo complex with its buildings scattered along the edge of the water. He parked behind a sparkling white high-rise, and Cindy pulled into the space next to his. When he got out of his car to meet her he said, "I'm on the fourth floor."

Cindy walked at his side, observing the scenery, which was gorgeous. Rich plantings abounded, with many palms and flowering shrubs contributing a riot of color.

"Did you think I would call you while I was gone?" Fox asked suddenly, and Cindy looked at him. He was watching her with that alert expression she had already come to know. It meant that the casual question carried more import than the listener could guess from his offhand tone. Was this a test?

"I know you were busy," she said carefully.

He looked away and dropped the subject. Cindy couldn't tell anything from his demeanor. She was getting mixed signals from him; on the one hand, he seemed to want her attention very much, but on the other, he acted as if any sign of possessiveness would cause him to bolt. He was a complex man and she knew that he would always defy easy categorizations.

Fox pushed open the outer door for her, and they entered the lobby. It was lush, with pearl-gray carpeting interspersed with walkways of rich terrazzo tile. Vivid contemporary paintings were mounted on a background of beige grasscloth walls, and hanging baskets of ferns were everywhere.

"Drew, this place is something else," Cindy said, staring unabashedly.

He flashed her a delighted grin. "Yeah, I know. Everybody who lives here is blue-chip, except for me. You should have seen the looks on the faces of the other happy home owners when I moved in with my three duffel bags of T-shirts and jeans."

Cindy got a sample of what he meant as a middle-aged couple passed by on their way out. They were extremely well-dressed, and the woman wore so much gold jewelry that it was amazing she was able to move at all. They both nodded stiffly at Fox, their expressions glacial.

"My next-door neighbors," Fox said out of the corner of his mouth to Cindy. He waited until they were out of earshot and added, chuckling, "They haven't decided whether I'm a hit man or a white slaver."

Smiling, unable to resist his relishing their confusion, Cindy said, "Why don't you just tell them what you do?"

"And ruin all the fun? No way," Fox replied, pressing the button for the elevator. "Besides, they would hardly regard my line of work as any better than their imaginings. The fact that they inherited all their money and don't work at all doesn't prevent them from looking down on those who do."

"Are you going to tell me how you wound up in this place?" Cindy asked archly, as the elevator arrived and they got into it.

"Dying of curiosity, aren't you?" Fox asked, shooting her a sidelong glance.

"Yes," she admitted, and he laughed, throwing his head back in a boyish gesture that made her want to kiss him.

"I'll tell you," he replied, pointing to his door as they got off the elevator. "About nine months ago I got a call from an oil company representative. The suite in this building was being used by one of their vice presidents, who had just absconded with one-and-a-half million of the company's funds. They were understandably anxious to locate him, and they offered me ten percent of that figure if I could bring him back."

He shrugged as he unlocked the door. "It wasn't my usual thing, more a missing persons case than anything else. The guy hadn't jumped bail; he'd just left. But I was intrigued and went after him. I finally found him a few months later in Rio, with a phony name, a phony passport, and a Brazilian mistress. When I turned him in, the company offered me this place in lieu of the fee. The crook wasn't going to be using it anymore, and it was worth about what they owed me, give or take a few grand. At first I thought I'd sell it, but I decided to stay when—"

"When you saw the effect your presence was having on the uptight tenants," Cindy finished for him, and he smiled at her.

"Smart girl," he said, and bowed her inside.

The apartment ran from front to back, with the entry hall leading straight ahead into the living room, and the kitchen and dining area on the left. To the right, off the living room, were the two bedrooms. The kitchen was galley-style, gleaming with space-age appliances, and had a counter that bordered the dining room directly next to it. The living room featured polished hardwood floors and a brick fireplace with an oak mantel. Through the sheer drapes she could see a balcony that ran along one end of the suite, with access from both the living room and the master bedroom.

Fox was standing next to her, waiting for her reaction.

"What can I say, Drew? It's spectacular."

"Notice anything unusual?" he asked, teasing.

"You mean the unusual lack of furniture?" she answered, and he nodded.

Aside from a metal card table in the dining area and a mattress visible through the door of the master bedroom, there wasn't a stick of furniture in the whole place.

"Looks like a bus stop, doesn't it?" he said cheerfully, waving her toward the single folding chair.

Cindy sat in it and looked around. "Why don't you have any furniture?"

He went to the refrigerator and got himself a beer, holding one up for her. She shook her head.

"Didn't think so," he said, smiling, and then answered her question. "My stuff from the old place was too worn out and beat up to bring here, so I decided I would get some new furniture. I gave the old junk away, except for what you see, but so far I haven't gotten around to buying anything." He saluted her with his can of beer. "Think how disappointed any potential burglar would be, going through all the trouble of breaking in just to find this ghost town." He grinned hugely, savoring the image.

"What's that?" Cindy asked, as a switch was thrown somewhere in the apartment, followed by a low, steady hum.

He shrugged. "Beats me. It's either the air conditioning, the air purification system, or the humidifier. This place has them all, not to mention a dozen switches on the stove that defy explanation. You need a pilot's license to operate it. You should see the owner's manual; it looks like the Manhattan phone directory."

Cindy laughed. She loved him in this mood: open, expansive, amusing. She watched as he took a deep swallow of his drink and then turned to look at her, his expression brightening.

"Hey, I have an idea. Why don't you help me buy some stuff for this place? We could shop for it together; it would be a kick."

"Me?" Cindy said.

"Sure, why not. You're a classy lady; you've got a lot of style. I'm sure you could pick out things that would fit. There's a place over on Del Rey Avenue that carries everything."

"Drew, Paula ordered her bed from there; it's very expensive."

"I've got money. It's taste I haven't got."

"Oh, Drew, don't be ridiculous," she said, shaking her head.

"I mean it. I'm no interior decorator; I have no idea what to buy. What do you say, will you help me?"

"Now?"

"No time like the present. Are you through for the day at the library?"

"Yes."

"Then let's go." He crushed the empty can and threw it in the trash as he headed for the door. Cindy had no choice but to follow. He locked the door after them and put his arm around her, hugging her to his side. It was the first time since he'd been back that he had touched her, and she felt a thrill of warmth from the contact.

"Do you charge a commission for your services?" he asked softly, as they headed for the elevator.

"My services are always free to a friend," she replied simply.

"Am I your friend?" he asked, looking down at her.

"I hope so."

"Count on it," he said firmly, and punched the button for the elevator.

Furniture Gallery was the sort of place where hordes of anxious clerks hovered over every customer, eager to boost their sales commissions. Cindy quickly saw that they would not be able to browse undisturbed, and so enlisted the aid of an elderly lady who didn't look too aggressive.

"What did you have in mind?" the clerk asked, looking from one to the other expectantly.

"Well, we're furnishing an oceanfront condo," Cindy explained.

"I have just the thing," the lady answered, leading them to a set of flowered chintz sofas with a matching armchair. "Perfect for a vacation home."

Cindy glanced at Fox, who rolled his eyes. In an undertone he said, "That stuff would be okay if I was planning on giving a lot of pajama parties."

Trying to keep a straight face, Cindy said, "Maybe we'd better be more specific. It's not a vacation place; it's a year-round home that happens to be on the water. And it's for him," she added, nodding at Fox.

"Oh, for the gentleman," the clerk said, beaming. "Something a little more masculine."

"That might help," Fox said evenly, and Cindy stepped on his foot. Hard.

The saleslady led them through a morass of various styles, trying to get a feel for what he liked. He seemed to express a preference for plain, functional furniture in quality woods, and they settled on a modern-looking dining-room set in bleached oak, with twin leather sofas and glass-topped tables for the living room. When the clerk began to wander aimlessly through the aisles, obviously exhausted, they decided to leave the bedroom set for another day. Fox went with her to the office to arrange a delivery date, and Cindy saw him slip her a folded bill when he thought no one was looking.

During the following week they had a hilarious time picking out the rest of the furniture, as well as pictures, lamps and knickknacks to complete the apartment. Cindy arranged her schedule to accommodate their shopping trips, and they became well-known at the Gallery in short order. Cindy had to correct several people who assumed they were married or engaged, and Fox looked on solemnly as she selected items with amazing rapidity. She had always worked on a budget, and it was fun to pick things just because she liked them, without worrying about the cost.

They spent a lot of time together, and by the end of it Cindy was so in love with Drew that she had forgotten what it was like not to know him. She hated to see the project end, but short of wallpapering the ceiling, there was nothing left to do. And something was bothering her. Since the day he met her at the library, Fox hadn't pressed her for anything more than a goodnight kiss. Although the atmosphere was rife with sexual tension, he did nothing about it, and Cindy didn't understand his restraint. Though he was affectionate in a general sense, stroking her hair, touching her face, he avoided more intimate contact with the same deliberate concentration with which he had once sought it. Cindy was relieved in one sense, but disappointed in another. She wanted Fox badly and wanted him to feel the same way. She needed his desire, and found that she missed the affirmation of it.

One night they were scheduled to go back to his apartment to accept delivery on the coffee tables. On the way Fox suggested they stop in Council Rock at a place that sponsored a happy hour every day for tired workers. It wasn't exactly Cindy's sort of thing, but she was willing to do anything he wanted. Once there it became clear that he had some business with the proprietor, because the man took him aside and they conducted a hushed conversation that Cindy couldn't hear. She strongly suspected that there was something about this venture that Fox didn't want her to know, and so she refrained from questioning him when he returned to their table with her glass of wine. He was silent as she drank it, staring into space and looking at her only when she spoke to him. She was about to ask him what was wrong when a disturbance at the bar caused them both to look up.

An Indian man was being forcibly restrained by the bartender. He was obviously drunk and quarrelsome, trying to break free and get at one of the patrons. He must have come in after them, because Cindy could see that Fox knew him and had probably been looking for him. Fox told her to wait for him and got up immediately, taking charge of the situation and helping the bartender usher the troublemaker toward the door. Cindy followed after him, worried, and as they passed her the drunk caught sight of her anxious eyes on Fox, who was dragging him toward the exit.

"Wait a minute, wait a minute," he said, eyeing her dazedly. "Is this your *shankree* girlfriend, Foxman? Walter told me all about her."

"Shut up, Evan; you're drunk," Fox said tightly. He turned to Cindy, his eyes furious. "I told you to stay put," he bit off between clenched teeth. "Go back to the table."

"This is the researcher, right?" Evan went on, ignoring Fox. He let out a loud guffaw. "I can imagine what research you're doing with my stud cousin here."

Fox turned pale. He took hold of Evan by the collar and hauled him through the entrance and into the street. Cindy stood rooted to the spot as the other patrons returned to their places, some of them glancing at her curiously. She was still motionless when Fox returned. He passed her and left money on their table, saying to her on his return trip, "We're leaving."

The owner stopped them on the way out to thank Fox for evicting Evan.

"Why didn't you tell me he would be like that?" Fox asked him angrily. "I would never have brought the lady if I had known."

"I didn't know either, Drew," the owner replied. "I just wanted you to talk to him. I thought he would be all right until closing time. But he's just been getting worse; you saw for yourself."

Fox nodded curtly, taking hold of Cindy's arm and guiding her outside. Once on the street he put his hands on his hips and took a deep breath, looking at her directly.

"What happened to your cousin?" Cindy asked gently.

"I got one of the other waiters to take him home," Fox replied. "I came here to try to save his job. The manager complained about him getting loaded at the end of the evening, before locking up. I thought I would be early enough to catch him sober, but I was wrong." He tensed visibly. "There's no excuse for what he said to you. I'm sorry."

"It wasn't your fault."

"Yes, it was. I should never have taken you with me. I just didn't want to..."

"What?"

"Leave you," he said simply, and Cindy's fingers closed around his arm.

"Is that Walter's brother?" she asked quietly, treading gently on sensitive ground.

"Yeah. He's a cliché, a drunken Indian." He snorted bitterly. "You're always asking me about my family. You saw a great part of it tonight, right?"

"Oh, Drew," she said, her heart going out to him, "I don't care about that."

"But I do," he said shortly.

"Drew, we'd better get back to your place," Cindy said quickly, seeking to divert him. "It's almost six, and the delivery is scheduled for six-fifteen—the last one of the day, remember?"

He nodded absently, going with her back to his car, but his mind was obviously still on what had happened inside. They beat the delivery van by only a few minutes, but when the things arrived he hardly looked at them, signing the receipt automatically and walking away. When the door closed behind the crew from the store he went to the balcony off the living room, opening the sliding doors and inhaling the evening breeze. Cindy watched him standing there, with her and yet alone, and she longed to make him feel better, to comfort him with her closeness. She knew that she loved him; what was she waiting for? She had waited long enough. He would be the first, and that was exactly as it should be. Emboldened by her decision, she walked over to him and stood behind him, touching his shoulder.

"Drew?" she said softly.

"Hmm?" He was looking into the distance over the water, barely listening.

She put her arms around his waist and kissed the back of his neck, moving her lips slowly and sensuously over the sensitive skin. She felt him shudder violently, and then he shrugged her off, so forcefully that she fell against the door.

"What are you doing?" he said hoarsely, whirling to face her. Then he saw that she had fallen, and rushed to help her, instantly contrite.

"Are you all right?" he asked, helping her up. "I didn't mean it, Cindy, you're such a flyweight that you just took off like a shot."

"Why are you doing this to me?" she demanded, slapping his hands away, almost crying. "Why are you treating me like this? At the beginning you wanted me so badly, and now when I so much as touch you, you throw me off as if I were repulsive to you. Don't you want me anymore?"

He closed his eyes. "I want you," he replied quietly. "Now more than ever. If you only knew how much."

"Then what is it? What has changed? You wanted to take me to bed on our first date."

"That was before I realized that you were..." He stopped, but not soon enough.

"A virgin," she finished for him. "That's it, isn't it, Drew? You don't want to make love to me now because you know you'd be the first."

His silence was her answer.

"How did you know?" she asked quietly.

"I knew at the lake," he replied. "I sensed you weren't afraid of me, but of the experience. And a girl like you gives herself, not sex."

"I want to give myself to you."

"Don't say that," he said, clenching his fists. "This is all wrong, *we* are all wrong, can't you see that? Wasn't your encounter with Evan tonight enough to convince you of that? He's my blood, Cindy, my family. That's what my life is like. You're too fine to be mixed up with somebody like me. Go back to Pennsylvania and marry some professor who'll read books and wear cardigans and understand those papers that you write."

"I don't want a professor. I want you. Now. Tonight."

He shook his head. "I can't take that responsibility."

"What responsibility?"

He met her eyes. "It would mean too much to you," he said quietly.

"And nothing to you?" she asked, her voice barely audible.

"I didn't say that!" he flashed angrily. "Don't put words in my mouth."

"Then spit it out, Fox," she replied. "Tell me what you mean."

"I mean that we've come to the end of the road," he stated flatly. "I can't give you what you want. That's it."

"No, it's not. If you won't say it, I'll do it for you. You see in our relationship a similarity to that of your parents, which ended so badly. I know I'm nothing like your mother; Eli told me that, but I'm *shankree*, an outsider, an 'other'. That's what it means, right?"

"We're too incompatible for something lasting, Cindy. Even you must see that."

"I don't see it, but even if I did, couldn't we go back as we were?" she asked, like a child crying for the return of childish dreams. "I was so happy being with you, and I know you were happy, too."

He looked down and sighed. "How long do you think that would last? I want you too much to keep my distance; it's taken all my willpower to stay away this long. We'd soon be faced with the same problem." He met her gaze and smiled sadly. "Give it up, princess. Someday your prince will come, but he won't be me."

Cindy blinked back the hot tears that threatened to spill onto her cheeks. "Then there's nothing more to say," she stated quietly. "I think I'd like to go home now."

He followed her to the door, and there was no conversation during the trip to his car. He drove to Paula's house in silence, while Cindy struggled to regain her composure. She wanted to break down and bawl like a four-year-old, but she wouldn't, she would *not*, do it in front of him.

When he got out to walk her upstairs, she stopped him.

"That won't be necessary," she said crisply. "I'm capable of getting to the door on my own."

"You're not going to as long as you're with me," he answered readily, taking her arm. "Creeps lurk in these hallways, don't you know that? I'll see you to the door, and that's final."

She had only been seeking to shorten the agony, but went with him unprotesting, her strength waning. When he bent to kiss her good-night outside the apartment, she turned her head, unable to bear it.

"One kiss," he said huskily. "Don't be mean, princess. I know I don't deserve generosity, but give me something to remember."

When she closed her eyes to accept his mouth, a tear slipped from her lash and onto her face. He kissed it first, and then her lips, so tenderly that it was like the first time.

"Don't cry," he whispered. "I'm not worth it. Someday you'll realize that this was all for the best. Goodbye, my princess."

He moved back from her, and when she opened her eyes again, he was gone.

Seven

A week went by, and the time of Cindy's departure from Florida was approaching. Her work was almost done, and she had to get back to Pennsylvania to teach an undergraduate intersession course at the end of the month. In truth, she was glad to be leaving; memories of Fox assaulted her everywhere, and it would be good to return to places where he had never been.

She told Paula what had happened because Fox would have been conspicuous by his absence. To Cindy's everlasting gratitude, and Paula's credit, the latter kept her mouth shut.

Cindy took advantage of a welcome distraction in the person of her thesis advisor, Richard Caldwell. He was in the area to do his own research and called Cindy, who had left Paula's number at the department office. They arranged to get together for dinner; Richard was always full of campus gossip, and Cindy looked forward to a few hours away from her paper and thoughts of her abortive relationship with Fox. She suggested the restaurant in Council Rock where she had gone with Paula on the day of her arrival. It was pleasant and not too expensive. As she dressed to meet Richard she wondered why she couldn't have fallen in love with someone like him, staid and solid and responsible. But although she liked Richard, there was no magic with him and never had been. He was a friend, and that was all.

When she entered the restaurant she saw that he was already seated. He stood and waved to her, and the hostess showed her to his table.

"Well, hello," he greeted her, pulling out her chair. "How's life among the natives?"

I could tell you a few things about the natives, Cindy thought. Aloud she said, "Fine. The work's been going great and I'm almost finished. How about yours?"

Richard needed no more encouragement to regale her with the details of his project, and as he talked Cindy studied his neat brown hair, his neat tortoiseshell glasses, and his neat button-down shirt. He looked the picture of exactly what he was; an amiable career academic whose intellectual curiosity was the ruling passion of his life. He was the polar opposite of Andrew Fox, and yet attractive in his own way. She knew several women at the university who were interested in more than his credentials.

"So I should have the bibliography ready in about two weeks," Richard was saying.

"That's wonderful," Cindy responded. "It sounds like you haven't been idle. So tell me, what's been going on at Penn?"

During drinks and dinner, Richard went on about various people they both knew, in particular their department head, who had been giving him trouble. Campus politics was a labyrinth Cindy usually sought to avoid, but on this occasion she drew him out, eager to lose herself in the lives of others. They had just ordered dessert when she looked up to see Fox and a young woman being seated on the other side of the room.

Richard's voice seemed to be coming from a distance. Cindy masked her reaction by taking a long sip of water, and then said, "Richard, I think I've changed my mind. I'm kind of full, and I'd rather not stay for dessert. Would you mind if we left now?"

Richard, understandably confused, nevertheless agreed. He called the waitress back and rescinded their order, asking for the check instead. Cindy made a quick exit and parted company with Richard in the parking lot, where she had left Paula's car. Paula was on duty at the hospital, and Cindy had to pick her up at seven that night.

Cindy was almost sick with jealousy. She had never cared enough about a man to experience the emotion before, and she was feeling the full force of its destructive effects as she drove back to Paula's apartment. Fox's female companion had been very pretty, a tall, statuesque brunette, and all the way home Cindy imagined him touching her, kissing her.

Stop it, she instructed herself severely as she unlocked the door. She was behaving childishly, and she knew it. These things happened to people all the time. Just because it had never happened to her before didn't mean she had to fall apart like a teenager disappointed in a first crush.

She changed clothes and read the newspaper, killing time until she went for Paula. The hospital lot was crowded, and Cindy maneuvered the car to the emergency exit, where Paula was waiting. She had decided not to tell her friend about seeing Fox, but the words rushed out of her mouth as soon as Paula had closed the passenger door behind her.

"You just saw him?" Paula asked.

"About an hour ago. In the Golden Door down in Council Rock. He was with some girl."

"And how do you feel about that?" Paula asked.

"Paula, I was so jealous that I disgusted myself. I saw him ordering a bottle of wine, and I wanted to go over there and pour it on both their heads."

Paula stared at her. "You? The woman who never returned a single social call from a man during our entire four years of college unless I dialed the phone first?"

"Me," Cindy confirmed miserably.

Paula sighed. "You must be in love."

Cindy stopped at a red light and bent her head over the wheel. "What am I going to do? He told me he didn't want to see me anymore, but somehow that didn't sink in. I'm still reacting as if he were my exclusive property, which he never was in the first place. I feel like I'm going crazy."

"Look, Cindy, I haven't told you this because I could tell that you didn't want to discuss it, but maybe letting you go was the greatest compliment Fox could pay you."

"What are you talking about?" Cindy asked, as the light changed and she drove ahead.

"Just this. He could have slept with you, used you for the time you were here, and then kissed you off when you left. He's behaving honorably by his standards. Do you see that?"

"I guess so," Cindy replied slowly. "I know he was doing what he thought was right. But it doesn't help the pain much. Seeing him with somebody else went through me like a shot."

"Welcome to the world of disenchanted lovers," Paula said wryly. "See what you've been missing while hiding out in that ivory tower? It looks kind of safe up there from where you're standing right now, doesn't it?"

Cindy didn't answer. She didn't have to; they both knew that Paula was right.

Paula had decided to give herself a home permanent and enlisted Cindy's aid in rolling up her hair and applying the lotion. The smell of ammonia permeated the apartment as she sat in the bathroom waiting for the required time to elapse. Cindy was trying to watch television when her already shaky concentration was interrupted by an abrupt pounding on Paula's door.

"Who on earth is that?" Paula called from her seclusion.

"Should I get it?" Cindy asked doubtfully, as the noise continued.

"Maybe we should call security," Paula suggested, as the outer door, which was unlocked, burst open. Fox barged through it, his expression agitated.

"Cindy? What's going on?" Paula demanded, emerging from the bathroom with her hair mired in tiny pink curlers. End papers stuck out in all directions from this arrangement, which was held in place by a mesh scarf tied at the back of her neck.

"Good God," Fox said, when this vision appeared. "What's all that on your head? You look like you're wired for sound."

"Never mind," Paula snapped. "What do you mean by banging on my door like that? I was about to call the police. Haven't you heard of doorbells?"

"I want to talk to Cindy," he replied flatly.

"And this is how you go about it? Maybe she doesn't want to talk to you."

"It's all right, Paula," Cindy said. "I'll see him."

"Are you sure?" Paula asked suspiciously.

"I'm sure."

She nodded. With a final outraged glance at Fox, retired to the bathroom, slamming the door loudly.

"She's crazy about me," Fox said, deadpan, and Cindy suppressed a smile.

"You can hardly blame her," Cindy said.

"You're right about that. Since your arrival, our relationship, which wasn't the best to begin with, has gone straight down the tubes."

Cindy looked at him levelly. "Perhaps you'll be good enough to tell me what all this is about?"

"You know what it's about," he answered tightly. "I saw you in the Golden Door tonight."

"Oh. I was hoping that you missed me."

He nodded sourly. "I can understand why. You didn't waste much time, did you?"

"I could say the same about you."

"Who was that guy?" he demanded. "How do you know him?"

"You have no right to ask me these questions," Cindy answered, turning away.

"I have every right," he almost shouted, his eyes blazing.

She faced him again, her anger rising to meet his. "And just how do you figure that?" She shook her head incredulously. "You gave me the gate not one week ago, and now here you are grilling me like a suspicious husband. *You* wanted to stop seeing *me*; that whole scenario was your idea. Where do you get off pulling this interrogation number?"

"I did not give you the gate," he enunciated clearly, his fists clenching and unclenching reflexively.

"Oh? What would you call it?"

"I did what I thought was best for both of us."

"Fine. You should be happy. Then why are you here?"

"You know why I'm here. I didn't like the looks of that guy."

Cindy couldn't help laughing. Richard might be mistaken for an earnest intern or a fledgling minister, but never a cloak-and-dagger type. Fox was really reaching.

"Don't be absurd. That guy, as you call him, is my thesis advisor, and already on his way home to Pennsylvania."

Fox looked mollified. "Oh. Then it wasn't a date?"

"I had dinner with a friend. Can we leave it at that? Now unless you have something further to say, I suggest you get out of here before Paula's remaining patience runs out."

He remained motionless, staring at her stubbornly.

"Did you hear me?" Cindy asked.

He exhaled sharply and dropped his eyes. She waited as he shifted restlessly, obviously trying to say something that was difficult for him.

He looked up again, and she felt the impact of his eyes with an almost physical jolt.

"Look, can we start over again? I've been missing you, and I think I made a mistake last week, saying what I did. Maybe we should give it another try."

Cindy's pulses leaped, but she maintained the outward appearance of calm.

"I don't know if that would be such a good idea, Drew," she replied carefully.

"Why not?"

"Because I don't think you've really changed your mind about us. You just saw me tonight, and you're reacting emotionally. The basic problem remains."

"Aren't we the sensible little miss?" he said acidly. "As logical as a computer. And just as cold."

"Logic is better than runaway romanticism."

"Oh, come on, get off it. You're just trying to punish me for last week. I hurt you, and you want to hurt me back."

"I don't operate that way, Drew," she answered quietly. "But I can't help it if you think I do."

"So your answer is no?"

She wanted to agree, but found that she couldn't. She needed to be with him so badly that it overrode caution and reason.

"What did you have in mind?" she hedged.

Encouraged, he said eagerly, "I play on a semi-pro jai alai team in Ocala. We have a game Friday night. You could watch me play and then we could go out afterward. Does that sound okay?"

She couldn't resist his childlike enthusiasm. He had missed her. He must have, to be so thrilled at her hint of acceptance.

"Okay," she said, and he grinned.

"I'll pick you up at seven," he said, heading for the door.

"Drew?" she called, as he reached for the knob.

He looked at her over his shoulder.

"What's jai alai?"

He laughed.

"You'll see," he answered, and left.

Watching jai alai proved to be an enlightening experience. A game invented by the Basques of Spain, it resembled handball, except that the players didn't hit the ball with their hands. They caught it in a mitt called a cesta and then threw it back. Fox's game was being played in an arena called a fronton and was the subject of mass betting among the spectators. Fox got Cindy a front-row seat, and she didn't care that she couldn't understand a thing going on in the court. Her eyes glued to Fox, she watched his lightning moves throughout the game, leaping to her feet and screaming with the other fans every time it was clear that he had scored. His team won, and afterward they went out with a group of players and their dates, or wives, until Fox took her aside during a lull in the music.

"Let's blow this joint," he said. "The dining room set we ordered arrived. Do you want to go over to my place and see it?"

This was clearly a pretext to get her alone, but Cindy wanted that as much as he did. She nodded, and he made their excuses to the group.

They went to his apartment and looked at the new furniture. They looked at the view. They looked at the newly installed carpeting in the hall. They avoided looking at each other. Finally Fox came and stood next to Cindy at the window. He touched her arm and she jumped.

"Yeah," he said huskily. "I know exactly how you feel."

Cindy turned to look at him. His hair was still slightly damp from his post-game shower, and it clung together at the ends in shiny tufts. He wore a green pull-over that heightened the color of his eyes, and his tan deepened the dusky shade of his skin to sepia. He was beautiful, exotic, infinitely desirable to the woman who saw in him the culmination of centuries of struggle and endurance. Maybe he wasn't perfect, maybe he wasn't even right for her, as Paula said, but she loved him, and that was all she knew.

Fox reached out and gently tucked her into his arms. "I can't fight this anymore," he murmured. "I want to make love to you, Cindy. Do you still feel the same?"

Cindy's throat tightened with unshed tears, and the right words would not come. He misinterpreted her silence, and released her, his face shadowed with a disappointment so deep he was unable to conceal it.

"No, huh?" he said, making an attempt to dismiss it lightly. "I guess I blew it. You should have told me that it was a one-time-only offer." He couldn't quite pull it off, and his shoulders slumped in defeat. "I'm sorry," he added quietly. "I'll take you home."

Cindy stepped forward and slipped her arms around his lean waist. With a sigh of complete surrender, she put her head on his shoulder and closed her eyes.

He understood and enfolded her once again. "Oh, princess," he said, in a voice that was not quite steady, "all those years in school and you still don't know what to say at a moment like this."

"I've never had a moment like this, Drew," she whispered. "I want to share it with you, only with you."

"And you will," he said fiercely, his grip tightening. "After I brought you home the last time you were here,

I thought, if I'm not the first, some other man will be. The idea drove me crazy. And then when I saw you with that guy in the restaurant...."

Cindy raised her head to look at him. "You have no rival in Richard, Drew. You have no rival in anyone."

She saw him draw a breath, and then he kissed her so urgently that she had to clutch his arms to keep from rocking back on her heels. He shifted position, clasping her with one arm and slipping the other under her knees. Cindy's feet left the floor as he picked her up and strode with her into the bedroom.

Fox set her gently on the bed, kneeling before her on the floor. Cindy had picked out the spread, the curtains and the rug, but everything looked new, as if she were seeing it for the first time. When Fox reached up to undo the buttons of her blouse, she shivered. His hand fell away, and he moved to sit next to her.

"Come here," he said. She relaxed into his arms. "Your teeth are practically chattering," he said into her ear. "It can't be the climate controlled temperature in this computerized apartment, so it must be me."

Cindy managed a small laugh.

"That's better," he said, a smile in his voice. "Who's afraid of the big bad wolf?"

"Fox," she corrected, and he chuckled.

"Look," he said, sitting up and cupping her chin in his hand. "Nothing will happen if you change your mind. Just say the word and we're both out of here."

Cindy met his eyes. "I don't want to go...it's just that..." She looked away. "Virgins are so much trouble, aren't they?"

"*You* are no trouble at all," he answered. "Listen to me now. We'll take it easy and go slow. If at any time you want me to stop, just tell me and I will."

"You will?" she said.

"Of course. I'm not a machine that can't be stopped once it's set in motion, and I don't want to rape you. I want to *love* you. It won't be any good for me unless it's good for you, don't you understand that?"

"I understand," she replied meekly, and he grinned.

"Now let's try this again," he said, and undid her buttons one by one, watching her face. She sat placidly and let him do it. He removed her blouse, and then her light cotton slacks. His eyes moved over her slowly when she was wearing nothing but her lace bra and panties.

"Your skin is beautiful," he whispered, bending to run his lips along her bare shoulder. "Like porcelain. I'm glad you don't have a tan."

"I can't get a good tan," she answered, her voice wobbling as his tongue probed the hollow of her throat. "I'm so fair I always burn."

"You are fair," he said huskily. "The fairest of them all." His mouth moved lower and found the swollen nipple that strained against its silken covering. The heat of his lips penetrated the cloth with such intensity that Cindy felt as if she were wearing nothing.

He sat up abruptly, pulling off his thin knit sweater. The sight of his naked torso brought back vivid recollections of seeing him working at his grandfather's. Then, he had been too far away to appreciate fully, but now he was close enough to see the pulse beating

strongly at the base of his throat. She reached out and
touched it, feeling the life coursing beneath her fingers, life as precious to her as her own. His skin glowed
with a soft patina of health, and the perfectly propor-
tioned muscles it covered contracted as she stroked him.
Her fingers trailed over his flat stomach, ribbed with
years of conditioning and etched with a random pattern of faint and newly healed scars.

"Don't hold back," he whispered, his lambent eyes
resembling those of the sleek animal for which he was
named. "You can trust me, princess. Do what you feel.
Do what you want."

With a strangled sound, half sigh, half moan, Cindy
put her arms around him and kissed his chest linger-
ingly, luxuriously. She rubbed her cheek on the smooth
surface of his shoulders and ran her hands down his
spare, sculptured back, surrendering herself to the experience.

"So many people have hurt you," she murmured,
gliding her lips over a thickened weal of pink scar tissue. "So much pain. Drew, how can you bear it?"

"It's my life," he responded softly, holding her to
him. "I am Indian. I accept."

Cindy pressed her mouth to one of his nipples, suck-
ing gently. He gasped and his hand tightened on the
back of her neck. She set her teeth on him, nipping
lightly, and he pushed her backward on the bed, loom-
ing above her. He twined his fingers with hers and raised
her arms above her head.

"You're a fast learner, Miss Warren," he murmured, kissing the corner of her mouth.

"First time lucky," she answered. "Lucky to be with you."

"I hope you'll always think so, princess," he said quietly, kissing her nose, then her brow. His lips returned to hers, and he kissed her deeply, moving to lie against her. Cindy explored the textures of his mouth: softness of lips, smooth wetness of tongue and slick hardness of teeth. He slipped his hands under her and unhooked her bra, pulling it off and tossing it on the floor. He pressed his face to her breasts instantly, closing his fingers around one and taking the hard peak of the other into his mouth. He groaned with satisfaction, and Cindy realized, through the drugged haze of her own pleasure, what it had cost him to approach her so cautiously.

He gave careful attention to her breasts, and then moved lower, kissing her abdomen. Cindy's shyness receded before a rolling wave of intense feeling that obliterated every other emotion. She lay supine as he caressed her ever more intimately, nudging her toward the fulfillment they both wanted, but sensitive to her least indication of resistance. When he slid his forefinger under the waistband of her pants, she stiffened automatically. He withdrew his hand immediately, shifting to cuddle her, switching moods to become the unthreatening protector once again.

"Relax," he murmured soothingly, rocking her to and fro. "There's no rush. We have all the time in the world."

He kissed her gently, and she sighed, unwinding visibly. He waited until he could feel that her desire was stronger than her anxiety and then set her back down, bending to kiss her thighs, the swell of her hips, the soft dimple of her navel. Before she knew what was happening she was lifting herself off the bed to help him strip away her last defense.

Cindy lay naked, and Fox's lips parted as he drank in the sight of her, his eyes moving greedily over every lovely inch.

"I wish you could see how you look to me," he whispered. "I'll never, never forget." In a gesture of homage, almost of worship, he stretched out next to her and pressed his burning cheek to her bare belly. His body radiated heat, and the flush staining his skin made him look more primitive than ever. His eyes were closed, and the curve of his lashes swept his cheeks like tiny black webs. Cindy rested her hand on his head, moving her fingers through the thick mass of his hair. He inhaled sharply, and then exhaled in a long breath. She heard it catch in the middle, like a sob.

He sat up abruptly, blinking rapidly, and stood to remove the rest of his clothes. She looked away until he joined her on the bed. He enfolded her, stroking the satiny slope of her spine. The shock of his nakedness was pleasant, and then intoxicating, as his legs moved between hers and she felt the hard strength of his body, the urgency of his desire. He kissed her everywhere, her lips, her breasts, caressing her from her fingers to her toes until she was clutching him, straining against him eagerly. She wound her legs around him, so anxious for union that she unconsciously moved into position.

He was trembling, but still in control. He slid his hands beneath her hips, where she could feel the imprint of each finger like a brand.

"This may hurt," he said hoarsely, on fire to bury himself in her, but still trying to shield her from all pain.

"I don't care," she moaned, no longer needing his restraint. She was all woman now, restless, seeking, digging her heels into the back of his legs. Her nails scraped his shoulders, slick with sweat, and she surged against him.

He entered her partially, and she grimaced, but made no sound. He waited, perfectly still.

"Are you all right?" he asked, fighting off the instinctive urge to continue.

Cindy opened her eyes to look at him, and in his gaze she saw the love he had never expressed in words.

"I'm fine," she whispered and kissed him. He kissed her back eagerly, and on his lips she tasted the salt of his effort to control himself.

"Then hold me tight," he said. She did so, and he thrust again. She gasped as he joined with her fully, and lowered his weight onto her, embracing her completely.

"Oh, Drew," she moaned. "I feel like part of you." Her head fell back and he settled against her, their bodies interlocked, a perfect fit.

"You are," he responded, moving within her so skillfully that she arched her back and her breath hissed between her teeth. "Now come with me."

"Anywhere," Cindy answered. "I'll go with you anywhere."

And she did.

Cindy awoke to the sound of running water. She was alone in the bed. Fox's scent was everywhere: in the sheets, on her skin, like a warm and musky perfume. She was drunk with it, and him.

She glanced at the clock. It was just after midnight; he had made love to her for a long time.

She got up and wrapped the sheet around her, wandering to the bathroom, the source of the noise. Fox was kneeling on the floor next to the tub, sprinkling salts into the rushing water and splashing them around to make suds.

He looked up and saw her in the doorway. "I'm running this for you," he announced, holding out his hand.

Obediently, Cindy padded to his side. He helped her out of the sheet and into the water.

"Be right back," he said, as she sank up to her chin in fragrant bubbles. She shrugged philosophically, and stretched, letting the wet heat soak into her bones. Her glance fell on the bottle of salts on the shelf above the tub. It was an expensive brand, and obviously not his. She tried not to think about the woman who had left it behind.

Fox returned with a tumbler half filled with amber liquid. "Brandy," he said, and handed it to her.

Cindy accepted it without thought, and then started to smile. The smile soon escalated into laughter. She grabbed a handful of foam and threw it at him. He stared at her.

"Goose," she said, and laughed again.

He put his hands on his hips.

"I've lost my virginity, Drew, not my mind. You're treating me like a psychiatric case."

His face fell, and then his mouth assumed the stubborn line she knew indicated trouble. He didn't like being laughed at, even by her.

"Well I don't know what to do for you," he said resentfully.

She raised her brows and looked him straight in the eye. "Don't you?" she asked.

Never a man to miss such a cue, he dashed to the tub and grabbed her, hauling her bodily out of the water. She kicked and flailed her arms, streaming water and suds onto the tile floor. Foam flew in all directions as he carried her, laughing and struggling, to the bed.

"I'm all wet!" she protested, as he tossed her onto the sheets and stripped off his jeans. "And covered with soapsuds."

"Cleanliness is next to godliness," he said piously, and jumped in with her. She settled down immediately as he pinned her under him, holding her still.

"What?" he said, teasing. "Nothing to say?"

"Nope," she answered, putting her arms around his neck.

"Okay," he said, feigning ignorance. "You're going to have to tell me what you want."

She squirmed, not comfortable with putting it into words.

"You know," she whispered.

He shook his head.

"Mm lf ti muh," she muttered.

"Can't hear you," he said, putting his finger in his ear.

She narrowed her eyes, fuming.

"Guess I'll be going," he sighed, and levered himself off her. She reached up and yanked him back down to her, where he collapsed, laughing.

"You're so funny," she said disgustedly.

"Still haven't heard the magic words," he said, shrugging, his grin roguish.

"Make love to me!" she yelled, and his eyes widened.

"Well why didn't you say so?" he asked, and kissed her.

She punched his shoulder, once, lightly. Then her fingers curved around his arm, and she kissed him back, ravenously.

"Wow," he gasped, raising his head. "I've created a monster. Are you sure you're new at this?"

"You know I am," she answered, pulling away.

"Don't get huffy; I was only kidding," he said mildly, holding her fast. "I just meant that you're a quick study, that's all."

"I always catch on to new concepts easily," she recited stiffly, and then heard what she had said. She giggled, and he covered his eyes with his hand.

"Give me a break," he moaned.

"You asked for it," she reminded him.

"So I did," he agreed, nuzzling her neck. He drew her against him, and she fitted herself to his body.

"Time for a quiz," he murmured. "We have to test how much you've learned in the past few hours."

"I'm ready," she sighed.

"Now pay attention," he began, and they took the test together.

In the morning, Fox woke Cindy with a kiss.

"Good morning, Sleeping Beauty," he said, as she yawned and rubbed her eyes. "Looks like I exhausted you."

"Are you the handsome prince who breaks the spell?" she asked, regarding him contentedly.

His face clouded. "I'm no prince, sweetheart. I thought I already made that clear."

"Well, handsome, anyway," she said, smiling, trying to joke him out of his sober reaction.

He stood up silently and lit a cigarette. She followed after him, reaching for his shirt and slipping it over her head. It drifted to her thighs like a mini-dress.

"What's this?" she asked, surveying the food he had put out on the dresser. "What time did you get up? Don't you ever sleep?"

"Not much," he replied, exhaling a stream of smoke. "It's a waste of time."

"Did you make all this?"

He shook his head. "No chance of that. I got it from the take-out place where I bought the picnic lunches. I've been keeping that deli in business for ten years."

Cindy bit into half of an English muffin and took a sip of the juice provided in a plastic container. "Don't you want any?" she asked him.

He nodded, stubbing out his cigarette and picking up a styrofoam cup of coffee. He regarded her thoughtfully over its rim, his eyes unreadable.

"Guess what I want to do after this?" she said, and he coughed.

"Please," he said, setting the cup down and closing his eyes in a parody of strained endurance. "You're going to put me in the intensive care ward."

Cindy went to his side and lifted his hand to her face, studying it. The long brown fingers had broad, spatulate nails. The veins on the back were raised to prominence by long years of physical activity. She turned it over and kissed the hard palm.

"I doubt it," she said, setting her teeth on the edge of his thumb.

"Okay," he sighed, allowing her to tug him toward the bed. "But when you see me in an oxygen tent, hooked up to a heart monitor, with those tubes running out of my arms, remember that I warned you."

"Yeah, yeah, yeah," she replied, unbuckling his belt.

He laughed, seizing her and kissing her hard. "You're like a kid with a new toy."

"And I need some further practice in using it," she answered, with a sly glance.

He took his shirt by its hem and yanked it over her head. "Practice makes perfect," he said.

They spent most of that day in bed. Fox answered the phone twice, disposing of the calls briefly. From the tenor of what she overheard, Cindy gathered that they were business. He obviously didn't want to talk about it in front of her. After the second call, he switched on his answering machine and turned off the bell.

Hunger drove them out that evening. Since his refrigerator yielded nothing but beer and lettuce, they decided on a restaurant and got ready to go. As they were leaving, Cindy asked, in a casual tone that failed to disguise her true feelings, "Drew, who was that woman in the Golden Door with you the other night?"

He shot her a sidelong glance. "I was wondering when you'd get around to asking me that."

"It's all right if you don't want to tell me."

He grabbed her hand and pulled her against him. "I'll tell you. That was Rosalie, Walter's wife. If you had hung around for another five minutes you would have seen him join us. It was her birthday."

"Oh," Cindy said in a small voice, feeling silly.

"I guess we both jumped to conclusions that night, huh?" he said, smiling down at her.

"I guess so," she replied, thinking that there was still no explanation for the perfumed bubble bath. But she didn't have the nerve to ask him about that. One thing at a time.

Fox had parked his car in the underground garage. He had found the back window jimmied the previous week and had taken this precaution against theft. They took the elevator to the basement, where they were very much alone, since it was an unusual time for departure. The workers had already returned home, and it was a little early for the evening traffic. Fox was walking a little ahead of her, and as he turned to put his arm around her, his expression changed from a slight smile to sudden alarm.

That was the last thing she saw before the world went black.

Eight

———

Cindy woke to semi-darkness, with a throbbing pain in her head. It took her several seconds to determine that she was in a hospital. Antiseptic smells drifted in from the corridor, where she could make out the curved bar of a nurses' station. There was a rustle of starched fabric, and she realized she was not alone.

"I see you're awake," a man in a white lab coat said. "Just let me take a look at those eyes." He took out a tiny light which looked like a fountain pen and shone it in her eyes.

"Drew," Cindy said hoarsely.

"Pupils look good," the doctor said, as if congratulating her on some achievement. "How's the head?"

He put the light back in his pocket and made a note on a chart.

"Where's Drew?" Cindy said louder, sitting up. Pain shot through her head like a bolt of lightning, and she dropped back to the pillow, trembling.

"I would advise against any sudden movements," the doctor said cheerfully, too late. "That's quite a concussion you have there."

"Is Drew all right?" Cindy almost screamed. At least she tried to scream. It came out like a croak.

"Mr. Fox is fine," the doctor said soothingly, answering the question at last. "Or he will be, once we get him patched up."

"Patched up?" Cindy repeated faintly.

He looked at her for the first time, as a person rather than a patient, and saw the depth of her anxiety.

"Mr. Fox was stabbed in the arm, and one of my colleagues is putting in the stitches right now."

"Stabbed," she whispered. "Oh, my God."

The doctor replaced the chart at the foot of the bed and then came to stand next to her. He patted her hand awkwardly.

"Don't be upset," he said. "Mr. Fox is an old hand at this sort of thing."

"Well I'm not," she mumbled, and he smiled.

"No doubt. But you shouldn't worry unduly about your friend. He's been with us before, you know. He shows up every few months with something like this."

Cindy was silent, trying to put it all together.

"Aren't you interested in what happened to you?" the doctor asked.

She nodded, and discovered that it hurt to do so. "Yes."

"Apparently one of the men Mr. Fox put back in jail got out on parole. He found out where your friend lived and waited for him in that garage area. When you passed, he jumped both of you."

Cindy listened, too appalled to comment.

"He chopped you on the back of the neck first," the doctor continued equably, as if reading the weather report, "to get you out of the way, and then went after Mr. Fox with a knife, slicing his arm. Mr. Fox knocked him out and then brought you here in his car, violating every posted speed limit in the process. He picked up a police escort of two squad cars and they all roared into emergency at the same time. And I understand that the admitting nurse was your roommate, and she put on quite a scene. It was all very colorful, I assure you."

"Paula," Cindy murmured. Oh, no.

"And," the doctor said, warming to his tale, "Mr. Fox punched out an orderly he thought wasn't tending to you fast enough. I must say he was more concerned about your welfare than the pint of blood he had lost along the way."

"You were there?" Cindy asked, glad that she had slept through it.

"Only for the last part. The punching out, I mean. I missed your dramatic arrival by a few minutes, but I heard all about it."

I'm sure you did, Cindy thought gloomily. "Is Paula still here?"

"The nurse? Oh, no, we sent her home with a pre-scription for tranquilizers. I'm sure she'll be in to visit tomorrow."

"What's wrong with me? You said it was a concussion?"

"In simple terms, yes. You sustained a blow that might have caused damage to the spine or the head. We'll be doing some tests for intracranial pressure and a few other things tomorrow. I'm Doctor Markel, by the way, and I'll be back to check on you in the morning."

"I want to see Drew. Can I see him?"

Dr. Markel shook his head firmly. "Absolutely not. You need your rest and so does he."

"What about tomorrow? Can I see him tomorrow?"

"We'll talk about it then. Now settle down and the ward nurse will be in shortly to take your vital signs."

Whatever they are, Cindy thought. She watched as Dr. Markel bustled out the door, closing it behind him, eliminating her view of the hall.

She lay back and stared at the ceiling.

There didn't seem to be anything else to do.

In the morning, she was shuffled around for various tests, which ranged from the uncomfortable to the ridiculous. Apparently she passed them all, because around noon they began making noises about discharging her.

She asked about Fox five times and was put off with a range of excuses. She was told that he was doing well, but that she still could not see him.

Paula arrived after lunch, carrying a plant bigger than she was. She took one look at Cindy and burst into tears.

"Stop crying, Paula, I'm all right. What is that, a baby tree?"

Paula put the bush down and pulled a wad of tissues from her pocket. "I couldn't believe it when they brought you in," she began. "You were out cold, white as a sheet, and Fox was covered with blood, yelling for us to take care of you. He looked like something out of a horror movie, even his hair was matted with gore. I thought you were dead, and he was dying."

"It's over, Paula. We're both all right."

"No thanks to him!" Paula said fiercely. "I knew he would be trouble. Didn't I tell you he would be trouble? He's dangerous, those people he chases are dangerous. That guy who attacked you really meant business, you know. When they brought him back to jail he said he didn't want to hire someone to go after Fox, he wanted the pleasure of taking care of him personally. 'Taking care of him.' His exact words." She shuddered.

"Calm down, Paula. You're getting hysterical."

"When I think," Paula ranted on, ignoring her, "of all the time I spent trying to get you out of those libraries and into a social life. And this is how you take my advice? By jumping from the reference stacks into knife brawls with hoods. By running around with Andrew

Fox, of all people! Even the *cops* are afraid of him."
She threw up her hands. "It's like going from singing
in a church choir to running guns for the mafia."

A nurse came in from the hall, glancing at Paula's
offering. "I see that Birnam Wood has arrived," she
said dryly. Paula threw her a dirty look.

"Time to take your pulse," she said, picking up Cindy's wrist.

"How is Andrew Fox?" Cindy asked her.

The nurse smiled. "You two should work up a rou-
tine. Every time I go in his room he asks about you."

"He might well ask," Paula sniffed. "He's the reason she's here in the first place."

The nurse glanced curiously at Paula. "Don't you
work down in emergency?" she asked.

Paula nodded. "I was there when the two of them
came in."

The nurse grinned. "Some show, huh?"

Paula turned to Cindy. "Your mother called, and I
had to make up a story about your absence. I didn't
dare tell her the truth or she would have been flying
down here to see you on the next plane."

"Thanks," Cindy said. "I appreciate it." By com-
parison with Cindy's mother, Paula was a rock, a bas-
tion of stability.

The nurse left, and Paula stayed until visiting hours
were over, settling down enough to discuss her budding
romance with the pharmacist and a few other mun-
dane topics. As soon as she left Dr. Markel appeared,
with his little light in his hand.

"Look at the ceiling," he commanded, and Cindy did. "Look at the floor," he said, and she complied.

He stepped back, satisfied.

"Well, young lady, I think you can go home."

A different nurse came in and handed him something to sign.

"I want to see Andrew Fox," Cindy said.

The doctor and the nurse exchanged glances.

"If you discharge me, I'll just visit him tonight," Cindy said reasonably.

"I don't think so," Dr. Markel said. "He doesn't want to see you. We have direct instructions not to permit you in his room, and we have to follow the wishes of the patient in these cases." He scribbled his signature and handed the clipboard back to the nurse.

"He won't see me," Cindy whispered, stunned. She couldn't believe it.

"I'm sorry," the doctor said, as the nurse looked on sympathetically. "But that's what Mr. Fox wants, and we can't risk upsetting him while he's still in our care." He eyed her thoughtfully. "Maybe he'll change his mind when he's feeling better."

"But why?"

Dr. Markel shrugged. "I don't know. He hasn't said much of anything really, except to ask about you. I must say it seems odd that he is so interested in your condition and yet doesn't want to see you for himself. But then, he's an odd fellow."

He nodded, dismissing the nurse, and she left the room.

"May I ask you a question?" the doctor said, startling Cindy out of her reverie.

"Yes."

"What's the story with Mr. Fox? You seem to know him better than most. He's a good-looking guy. Smart too, from what I can see. Why does he have to make his living getting banged up like a boxer in a two-bit smoker?"

"I think he likes it," she murmured, more to herself than to him.

"Beg pardon?" Dr. Markel said.

"He likes the danger, the excitement. Not knowing what's going to happen from day to day."

The doctor shook his head. "I don't understand that."

"Neither do I. But that's what makes him different from you and me."

"From most people, I would guess," Dr. Markel said practically. He folded his arms and surveyed her critically. "Now our usual discharge hours are in the morning, but if you'll sign youself out, I'll let you go as soon as you can pack your things. You'll need a ride home."

"I'll call Paula," Cindy said, reaching for the bedside phone.

The doctor headed for the door. On his way he paused and said, "Miss Warren? Good luck with your adventurous friend."

Cindy nodded and picked up the phone.

Cindy had almost managed to convince herself that there was some mistake, until she called the hospital the following day and was told that Fox still would not see her.

Paula entered the room as she was replacing the receiver.

"No change?" Paula asked.

Cindy shook her head.

Paula sighed. "Well, I was hoping things would improve, but since they haven't I might as well give you this now." She went to the coat closet and returned with a large gift box. "This came for you while you were still in the hospital. It's from him."

Cindy stared at the package. "How do you know?"

"I saw the receipt when it came. His name was on it, he ordered it by phone."

"What is it?"

"I don't know," Paula said, annoyed. "I didn't open it."

Cindy took the box and undid the cord, pushing aside the layers of tissue paper after she removed the lid. It contained a cornflower blue dress, just right for her pale hair and eyes, in her exact size. There was a card enclosed. She slit the envelope with her fingernail. Inside, on a plain background, was the drawing of a tiny fox face.

She showed it to Paula. "Why would he be sending me a dress?"

Paula shrugged. "I guess to replace the clothes you were wearing when you were attacked. Fox's blood got all over them. Didn't you realize that you were discharged in the things I had brought you?"

Cindy had been so disturbed by Fox's refusal to see her that she hadn't noticed what she was wearing.

"He must have had the delivery man stop by the hospital so he could insert the card," Paula mused.

The more Cindy thought about the gift, the angrier she got. "Paula, do you know what this is?" she asked, her mouth a tight line.

"A dress?" Paula said, stating the obvious.

"No. This is goodbye, the kiss off, the statement of farewell. He has decided for some reason or other that he doesn't want to see me again, and this little item is supposed to do the trick."

"Well," Paula began hesitantly, "maybe it would be best, in view of what's happened, just to let it go...."

Cindy threw the box across the room.

"I guess not," Paula amended quickly.

"The coward!" Cindy spat. "Well, they have to discharge him sooner or later, he can't avoid me forever."

Paula picked up the dress and folded it on a chair.

"If he wants to say goodbye, he'll have to do it to my face," Cindy said furiously. "When he gets out, I'll track him down and strangle him with that bloody dress!"

Paula waited until Cindy had stalked down the hall and into her bedroom. Then she sank onto the sofa and closed her eyes.

Who would have thought that shy, bookish Lucinda had it in her?

Fox was discharged from the hospital the next morning. As soon as Cindy got word from the information desk, she took Paula's car keys and left her a note. Paula had worked the night before and was still sleeping.

Cindy drove to Fox's condominium with a lot on her mind, the least of which was Dr. Markel's warning about driving. She didn't seem to be experiencing the dizziness or blurring of vision that he had discussed, so she forged ahead, more concerned about her showdown with her lover than the state of her health.

Next to her on the passenger seat was the box containing the blue dress. She eyed it as if it were a toad. He was going to be very sorry he ever came up with the idea of sending it.

She walked through the rarefied air of the lobby in Fox's building as if she belonged there. Luckily the security guard remembered her from her previous visits and waved her on. Cindy was working herself into fine mettle as she ascended to the fourth floor, and she rang the bell with the dress box under her arm like a crossbow.

A middle-aged woman answered the door. Startled, Cindy stammered that she wanted to see Mr. Fox.

"I'm the cleaning lady," the woman answered. "Mrs. Hallam, just hired last week. Mr. Fox ordered up a whole houseful of new furniture, and then discovered that it has to be dusted." She chuckled at her own joke.

Cindy smiled wanly. "Yes, I know. Could you tell him that I'm here and would like to see him? My name is Cindy Warren."

"Oh, he's not at home," Mrs. Hallam said, shaking out her dust rag. "I'll be happy to leave a message."

"Not at home?" Cindy said. "He was just discharged from the hospital this morning."

"Huh," Mrs. Hallam said disgustedly. "You didn't think that would nail his feet to the floor, did you? He no sooner marched in here than he marched out again, still wearing a sling on that bad arm."

"Do you know where he went?"

Mrs. Hallam looked her over suspiciously. "I don't know if I should say."

"Please, Mrs. Hallam. It's very important. I really have to see him today."

"Are you the little lady who picked out all this stuff?" Mrs. Hallam asked, gesturing expansively at the apartment behind her. "Mr. Fox talked about that."

"Yes, I am."

Mrs. Hallam nodded. "He told me he was going out to that property his uncle owns at some lake. Do you know where it is?"

"Thank you, yes, I do. I really appreciate the information. It was nice meeting you. Goodbye." Cindy was off down the hall again, leaving Mrs. Hallam to stare after her, shaking her head.

The drive to the lake seemed to take much longer than it had when she was with Fox, and she got lost once when she took a wrong turn. She hadn't been paying much attention to the route on her previous trip. But she recognized the scenery on the road to Eli's house, and as she passed it she remembered his invitation to come and see him. It looked like she never would.

She continued down the road, and it wasn't long before she saw Fox's pickup in the distance. She pulled up behind it and got out of the car, lifting the dress box into her arms again. She was really tired of carrying it around with her like a cardboard albatross, but it appeared that she would be relieved of her burden soon.

She heard a series of reports, sounding very loud in the wooded stillness. They continued, getting louder as she picked her way through the trees toward the shore of the lake. When she broke through the ground cover and into the clearing, she saw Fox about two hundred feet ahead of her, firing a gun.

He was taking target practice. He had set up a makeshift fence along the water, and was methodically shooting beer bottles off it into the dirt. His stance didn't waver and he didn't look at her. He never missed.

Cindy watched him undetected for a while, and then when he paused to set up new targets she called out to him. He spun around and stared at her, waiting silently as she walked across the grassy shore to his side. He didn't say a word.

"Hello, Drew," Cindy said when she reached him, with a calmness that surprised her. "How are you feeling?"

"Stabbed," he said shortly, and she smiled thinly.

"I see that. I like your sling. It gives you a decidedly piratical air."

"You mean more than usual?" he responded, and then added, "How did you find me?"

"I went to your place and your cleaning lady told me where you were. Does your doctor know you're out here doing this?"

"My doctor doesn't know a stethoscope from a stapler."

He obviously wasn't going to make this easy for her, so she decided to get it over with as quickly as possible. "I came to return this to you," she said flatly, and extended the box toward him.

He looked at it, then at her, making no move to take it. She bent and set it on the ground.

He watched her, rubbing his cheek with the back of his uninjured arm, the gun dangling loosely from his fingers.

Cindy shuddered. "Would you mind not waving that thing in my face?" she said sharply. "I hate guns."

Fox tucked it into the waistband of his pants. "So do I, but I find it necessary to be proficient with them in my line of work." He waited a couple of beats and then said, "Why don't you want the dress?"

"I prefer memories over material things," she said simply, and she saw the impact of her statement sink in.

"Are you all right?" he asked tightly.

"I am, although you would have no way of knowing it."

His eyes flashed. "I was in touch with that Dr. Markel the whole time you were in the hospital!" he said angrily. "Right up until the minute you were discharged."

"Why wouldn't you see me while you were there?" she flared back at him.

He looked away from her. "I thought it best to leave you alone. You were hurt twice because of me; I'm obviously not good for your health."

"I see. And it never occurred to you that I might be worried about *you*, that I might want to see for myself that you were okay?"

He wouldn't meet her eyes. "I'm sorry, Cindy. I'm sorry about all of it."

"*All* of it?" she asked, emphasizing the first word.

He knew exactly what she meant. "All of it," he repeated. "Getting involved was a mistake. Next time you might not be so lucky. Next time you might wind up in the morgue."

His voice was so cold, so distant, that it was hard for her to believe this was the same man who had made such passionate love to her only a few days before.

"All right, Drew," Cindy said. "I can't say I'm surprised. This is precisely the reaction I thought I would get from you. I know you very well, I find. I can predict your moods like the rising of the sun."

He looked at her then, his light eyes measuring, wondering whether she would make a scene.

"I'm going," she announced. "But before I do, I want to say something to you, and I want you to listen."

He didn't move, and his expression didn't change.

"I'm sure you've convinced yourself that you have the noblest of motives in sending me away. You can tell yourself that you're protecting me, and you may actually believe that. You can tell yourself that it's because of your parents, and believe that's valid too. But the truth is you're scared."

He straightened slightly, and his lips parted.

"I've gotten to you, haven't I, and that frightens you. Everybody told me how you acted when you thought I was really hurt, and that behavior doesn't lie. You care about me, and you were wild when you thought something had happened to me. Now you're pulling back from that and running in the other direction."

He lifted one shoulder slightly. "You can think that if it makes you feel better," he said evenly.

She shook her head. "Such a tough guy. You forget who you're talking to, Drew. I know you, remember?"

"You don't know anything about me," he replied.

"Don't I? You dashed back here to your childhood hangout to play with your little gun because it was easier than facing the feelings you have for me. Physically, you're ready to take on anything and anybody, but emotional intimacy terrifies you."

He didn't answer, his jaw clenched so tightly that the little muscles along its edge were jumping wildly.

Cindy sighed with resignation. "I've tried, Drew. I can't try any more. I love you, but I have had enough. Goodbye."

She turned her back and walked toward the trees.

He made no attempt to follow her.

Nine

Five days later Cindy was in the guest room packing to go home when Paula knocked on her door.

"Come in," Cindy called.

Paula entered, still in uniform, unpinning her hair from its severe workday style. "I saw your foxy friend this afternoon," she announced without preliminary.

Cindy looked up from folding a sweater into the suitcase set out on the bed.

"He stopped by the outpatient clinic for a checkup on his arm," Paula said. "I ran into him in the hall."

"Is he all right?" Cindy asked.

"He's fine, Cindy. Stop worrying. It'll take a silver bullet to finish him off."

"You're not amusing me, Paula," Cindy said. She tucked a set of underwear into the liner pocket. "I hope you behaved yourself."

"Don't look at me like that," Paula said. "I was civil to him." She folded her arms and leaned against the doorjamb. "He asked me when you were going back to Pennsylvania."

"Did you tell him?"

"You bet I did. I wanted to make it clear that you would be on your way very soon."

"Trying to get rid of me?" Cindy asked, with a faint smile.

Paula snorted. "If only that were your problem. Are you going to get over this, or what?"

"I have to, don't I? There's little choice involved."

"That louse," Paula said bitterly. "I could kill him."

Cindy shook her head wearily. "It's not his fault, Paula. I knew what he was like when I started with him; he never misled me. And despite everything, it was worth it."

"Do you mean that?"

"Yes, I do. When it was good, it was wonderful, and I wouldn't have missed that for anything. I just took a gamble and lost. That happens, doesn't it?"

"It happens all the time, to me," Paula answered sadly.

"It will be easier once I'm back at work," Cindy said with assurance. "I have nothing to do here now that the research is finished. Once I'm teaching those undergraduates, listening to their problems and trying to untangle their schedules, I'll be able to forget."

"Do you really think so?" Paula asked doubtfully.

Cindy sighed. "No, Paula, but I'm trying to be brave and you're not helping me," she said, irritated.

Paula shot her a look and they both laughed.

"Well, at least you haven't lost your sense of humor," Paula observed.

"The last refuge of the broken-hearted," Cindy said.

"You love him very much, don't you?"

"I think I always will. But I can't change what's happened; I have to live with it." She pointed to a pair of slacks hanging on the back of the door. "Hand me those, will you?"

Paula gave them to her and said, "What time is your flight tomorrow?"

"Three-thirty in the afternoon. You'll be on duty, right? I'll have to call a cab."

"Don't be ridiculous, to go that far it will cost a fortune. I have several people who owe me favors; I'll switch with one of them. Let me make a few calls."

"Thanks, Paula. I'm sorry about the timing, but it was the only flight I could get."

"No problem," Paula called, walking into the hall where Cindy heard her dialing the phone. Low tones of conversation followed while Cindy finished her packing and snapped the suitcase shut.

"I'm off again," Paula announced from the doorway. "Have to pull the night shift to clear the day tomorrow."

"Are you sure that's all right? Won't you be tired?"

"I'll have two days off to rest," Paula replied. "I'll
take a quick shower and change." She paused in mid-
stride. "I hate to leave you here alone."

Cindy smiled with a wry awareness of her situation.
"You're not my babysitter, Paula. I'll be fine."

Paula went into the bathroom, and Cindy sat on the
edge of the bed, looking around at the room that had
been her home for several weeks. It was barren now,
empty of her personal items, like a hotel room when the
guests have left.

At that moment, it seemed the perfect complement to
her desolate soul.

After Paula left, Cindy tried to read some of the
glossy magazines that Paula bought in stacks of five.
The articles on miracle diets and the latest makeup
techniques failed to hold her interest, and she switched
on the television set. The schedule offered nothing but
situation comedies full of unfunny situations and
canned laughter, and she shut it off again in frustra-
tion. Finally she put on a local FM radio station, turning the volume up on the rock music that filled the
apartment. She felt warm in the enclosed rooms and
opened the outer door to the screen. It was a cool night,
and Paula hadn't turned on the air conditioning.
Drinking in the fresh air that flooded in from the hall
like a tide, Cindy began to hum along with the singer
whose voice canceled the silence and lifted her spirits.

"I can't hold back; I'm on the edge," she sang as she
started to dance, which she often did when alone. Too
reserved to perform in public, she liked to fling herself

about when no one was looking. She indulged her need for self-expression and got the benefit of the exercise at the same time. She soon became overheated trying to keep pace with the driving rock beat and paused between songs to strip to her chemise, tossing her clothes on the sofa.

A new number began, and she joined in with it. She shimmied and spun around, carried away by the music, lost in the throbbing drums and wailing guitars. It was bliss just to move, not to think, to feel her heart beating, blood pumping, and the air filling her lungs. She was alive, and that, at least, was something to celebrate.

Cindy was so absorbed in what she was doing that when she whirled past the door and caught sight of a figure there, she stopped cold, gasping with shock. Her eyes widened and the back of her hand went to her mouth. It was Fox.

She had no idea how long he'd been there, but from his expression, it was a while. He was breathing hard, his broad shoulders rising and falling, his face filmed with a fine sheen of perspiration. The fever pitch of his excitement flowed from him to her in potent wordless communication.

Cindy stared at him, mesmerized.

He pushed the screen door open and stepped through it, never taking his eyes from hers. He kicked the storm door shut with his foot and locked it without looking at it. As he passed the stereo he shut it off.

He was wearing a blue cotton shirt, open at the throat, with a turquoise amulet on a silver circlet around his neck. It was the first Indian thing she had ever seen on him, and it glowed like a sapphire against the honey-bronze background of his skin. His jeans, as always, fit him like a sheath, clinging to his slim hips and powerful legs with flattering precision. His feet inside the battered brown moccasins were bare.

Cindy took a step toward him, forgetting that she wore nothing but a silken teddy, forgetting everything but the miracle of his presence. When he saw that she wasn't going to send him away, he covered the remaining distance between them in a second. He caught her to him in an embrace so powerful that it lifted her bodily into his arms.

He just held her for a few moments, savoring the sensation, and then knelt, lowering her to the floor. He looked at her for a long, breathless beat, then ran his hands over her body from shoulders to knees, molding the damp silk to her slender form. Cindy's lashes fluttered, and then her eyes closed.

Fox slipped the straps of the sleek ivory chemise down her arms, and then pulled it from her body, tossing it aside. He bent and encircled her waist with his hands, laving the tip of each breast with his tongue. Cindy sank her fingers into the wealth of hair at the back of his neck, holding his head against her. When he finally sat up, she clutched at his shirt, desperate to maintain contact.

He put her hands aside gently and took off his shirt as she watched through heavy-lidded eyes. When his torso was bare she reached up and caressed him, moving her palm from pectoral to bicep, admiring his beauty. His large fingers covered her smaller ones, and he pushed her hand down his muscular midsection to his thigh. When she touched him he closed his eyes and sighed so deeply that it echoed in the stillness of the room

He was motionless for a time, absorbing the feel of her hands on him. Growing impatient, she put her arms around him and tugged him toward her. Then he stood and removed his pants, while she shifted restlessly, anxious for his return.

When he joined her again, she put her arms around his neck and received him eagerly. He kissed her for the first time since he had arrived, his mouth full and warm on hers, and entered her at almost the same moment. Tears gathered in the corners of Cindy's eyes, and she turned her head, squeezing her lids shut to hide them. She knew that this was his farewell. She would never have this with him again.

It was over quickly; they were both too hungry to go slow. At the end, exhausted, they fell asleep immediately. Cindy's final impression was of Fox surrounding her, of being pinned to the earth by his sweet weight.

When she woke up, Fox was gone. Her head rested on a throw pillow from the sofa, and he had brought the quilt from the guest room, covering her with it. Her chemise was folded in a neat square on the chair by the door.

Cindy got up and, dragging the quilt after her, looked for a note. There was none to be found, but she hadn't really expected one. Dissatisfied with their brittle goodbye at the lake, he had come at the last moment to do it properly, to say with his body what he would never put into words.

Cindy glanced at the clock. Paula would be home soon. She pushed her hair back from her face, and, trailing the quilt like a child dragging a teddy bear, went into the bathroom to take a shower.

When Paula returned from work she found Cindy sitting cross legged on the sofa, wearing a bathrobe, and staring into space.

"Oh, oh," Paula said. "I know that look. He was here, wasn't he?"

Cindy nodded. "Paula, I'm such a fool. I had made up my mind to forget him, and when he showed up here tonight, it all went right out of my head. He didn't even have to say a word." She covered her face with her hands. "I feel like an idiot."

Paula sat next to her and patted her arm. "You're not a fool, Cindy. You're in love."

"I used to think I was so strong," Cindy went on. "But it was just because I didn't know. I didn't realize what it was like to feel this way." She shook her head slowly. "Fox is the strong one."

"I don't know about that," Paula replied. "He seems to be having a lot of trouble letting you go."

"He may be having trouble, but he'll do it," Cindy said.

"You're very certain."

"You'll see," Cindy said sadly, and she was right.

In the morning, Paula seemed to be waiting for the phone or the doorbell to ring. But as the hour of their departure for the airport approached and there was no word from Fox, she gradually realized that Cindy had been correct.

"I can't believe he's not going to stop you," Paula said to Cindy as they loaded her bags into her car.

"It's all right," Cindy said to her friend, who seemed more upset about it than she was. "I've accepted it. Now let's get going before I miss the flight."

They didn't hit much traffic on the way, and Cindy was early for the plane. Paula hung around morosely, staring up at the flight board and then at Cindy, her expression uncomfortable.

"Why don't you go?" Cindy finally said to her. "There's nothing you can do, and you must be tired. I'll be fine."

"Are you sure?" Paula asked, obviously relieved.

"Positive."

Paula embraced her. "I'm really sorry it didn't work out with Fox," she said. "I know I've said some bad things about him, but if he's what you want, you know I'd like you to have him."

"It's okay; I understand."

Paula smiled at her with misty eyes. "At least you got your work done. It's hard to remember that was the real reason you came here."

"Sometimes it is for me, too," Cindy replied, her tone wistful.

"I'm going to miss you. It was like being back in school again," Paula said, sniffing.

"Without the dormitory food," Cindy answered, and Paula laughed.

"And the hissing radiator," she added.

"And the guy who called at three A.M. every Friday night and breathed into the hall phone. Remember him?"

Paula groaned. "How could I forget? After we stopped answering the phone he started sending letters to the mail proctor, who just happened to be me."

They looked at each other, delaying the separation with small talk. They could never recapture a happy past that had fled down the corridors of time.

Paula hugged Cindy quickly again, and said, "Write or I'll kill you." Then she stalked off in the direction of the main doors, not looking back.

Cindy watched her leave, and then filed through the security check, dutifully producing her wristwatch when it set off the alarm. Then she sat in the lounge clutching her boarding pass, wondering how she was going to get through the rest of the day, the week, the month.

She leaned back in the seat and closed her eyes. She didn't open them again until the public address system announced the boarding of her plane.

Ten

___

Two weeks crawled by. Cindy submitted her paper and assumed her teaching duties, which failed to fill up her time in the way that she had hoped. She had enough free hours in which to miss Fox and rethink every moment she had spent with him. She kept telling herself that her state of mind would improve, but she didn't actually believe it. Like the human quarry that Fox chased, her heart had been stalked and captured.

She was the first person in the department on Thursday morning, and, after pausing in the lounge to make coffee, she unlocked Richard's door with one hand, balancing a stack of books with the other. Her briefcase was clutched under the arm that pushed in the door.

She took one look inside the office and screamed. All her burdens crashed to the floor.

There was a man sprawled on the carpet behind the desk.

Cindy thought briefly of security, and then realized that the guard was at the other end of the building and there was nobody else around. She was backing out when the man sat up and regarded her sleepily, awakened by the noise.

It was Fox. He pushed his hair out of his eyes and yawned.

"Hi, princess," he said, as if she had just encountered him in the checkout line at the grocery store.

"Hi!" Cindy exclaimed. "That's all you have to say? What on earth are you doing here? And how did you get in?"

"I broke in last night," he said casually, unfolding the jacket he had used for a pillow. "You should have that lock changed. I jimmied it in about three seconds, and then reset it once I got inside. Not very safe for all of your research, right?"

"Look," Cindy said, trying not to lose her temper, "suppose you tell me why you broke in at all. I presume you still know how to use the telephone?"

"Your number is unlisted," he answered, rising to his full height and stretching. "What a hard floor in here. Got to watch that. It could give you flat feet."

Cindy could feel herself mentally counting to ten. "You have my address," she said.

He shook his head, looking a little sheepish. "No, I don't. Paula wouldn't give it to me."

Cindy stared at him.

"I asked her for it, twice, and she said that I'd get the keys to the pearly gates before I got your address from her."

Cindy grinned. That sounded like Paula. "Now why do you imagine she said that?" Cindy asked him.

"She seems to think I treated you badly," he answered, his green eyes seeking hers.

"And what do you think?"

"I think I treated you badly," he said quietly.

That gave Cindy a moment's pause. She cleared her throat and asked, "How is Paula?"

"The same as ever. Mad at me."

"Good for her," Cindy said crisply.

He fidgeted with the blotter on Richard's desk. "Does that mean you're not going to listen to me?"

"That depends upon what you have to say," she replied, forcing herself to remain on the other side of the room. She wanted to run to him and fling her arms around his neck, but that would never do.

"Do you know why I came to see you the night before you left?" he asked abruptly.

"Why don't you tell me?"

"I knew that you were going, and I couldn't stay away. I had to be with you that one last time."

"And you were."

His expression softened, and his voice changed. "I can still see the way you looked, dancing all by yourself. You would never let go like that if you knew someone was watching."

"I let go," Cindy replied. "I let go with you."

Fox lowered his eyes. "Does that mean I bring out the worst in you?"

"The best, I would have said."

He drew a breath, then exhaled slowly. "That's why I'm here," he said. "Because we bring out the best in each other."

Cindy watched him, hardly daring to hope. He had disappointed her so painfully before.

Richard chose that inopportune moment to arrive at his office. He looked from Cindy to Fox and his mouth fell open.

"Hi, Richard," Cindy said quickly. "This is Andrew Fox; I met him when I was down in Florida. Drew, my thesis advisor, Richard Caldwell."

The two men shook hands, and Richard tried not to stare at Fox's wrinkled clothing or the backpack dangling by its strap from his arm.

"Drew, why don't we go down to the lounge and talk," Cindy said pointedly, taking his hand and practically dragging him into the corridor. "Richard, I left those notes you wanted on your desk."

Fox followed her down the hall, oblivious to the stares of the arriving employees. He was like an exotic bird in a covey of sparrows.

"Just go inside," Cindy said to him. "I'll be right with you."

She hurried down to the secretary and told her to greet her class and give them a reading assignment. Then she dashed back to the lounge, where Fox was drinking coffee and reading the notices posted on the bulletin board.

"Somebody's selling three dozen used tennis rackets for seventy-five dollars," he announced to her. "You ought to take advantage of that one."

"I have to make this fast," she said. "My class will be coming in soon."

He turned to look at her, and his face was expressionless. "I'm sorry if I interrupted your schedule," he said stiffly.

"Come on, Drew, be fair. I have work to do here, and I didn't know you were coming."

"All right," he said. "I'll be quick. I'm here because I can't live without you. I've tried, and I can't do it."

"You sound annoyed about it," she observed, almost whispering. She wanted to ask him to repeat it. Had he really said it?

The outer door opened and Rachel Clarkson came in, carrying a stack of papers. When she looked up and saw the two of them, her eyes darted back and forth, seeking explanation.

"Do you mind?" Fox asked, displaying his most charming smile. "I am trying to talk to this young lady." He ushered a stunned Rachel back out the door. Rachel was the worst gossip in the department; Cindy knew that the story would be legend by five o'clock that day.

"Drew, you can't keep throwing people out of here," she said, when he returned. "This is the department lounge, for heaven's sake."

"Really? I thought it was Grand Central Station." He sighed with exaggerated patience. "All right. Where can we go?"

Cindy thought about it with a mind too dazzled by his latest admission to have a clear grasp of anything. "The catalog room should be empty."

"I'm not even going to ask what a catalog room is. Lead on."

She took him through the office maze and out into the classroom corridor.

As they passed her class, which was filling up, Cindy told him to wait for her.

She went inside and confronted her students, who were groaning when they saw the reading assignment written on the blackboard by the secretary. They quieted when they saw her take her place in front of the podium.

"We thought you wouldn't be here," Brian Talbott said. "What's with the busy work?"

Cindy looked at them for a few moments, and then said, "Class dismissed."

No freshman class ever argues with that. Whooping their delight, they were gone in seconds, brushing past a grinning Fox, who greeted her with, "You can handle my classes anytime."

"That was very irresponsible of me," she said faintly. "I'll have to make it up later."

"Worry about it tomorrow," he instructed. "Right now we have more important things to take care of. Where's the catalog room?"

Cindy took him there and unlocked the door. Once inside, he pulled her into his arms and kissed her until she was breathless.

"Wait a minute," she said, holding him at arm's length when she finally managed to break away. "You're doing it again."

"Doing what?" he asked, seeking her mouth with his.

"Making love to avoid facing our problems."

"I'm here. We have no problems."

"Yes, we do. Why did you let me come back here, Drew? Why didn't you do anything about us when I was leaving Florida? Is this just going to be more of the same, seesawing back and forth? We'll have a great time until you get scared and run off again?"

He released her, his face set. "Boy, did you get tough all of a sudden."

"That's what happens when you cry yourself to sleep every night over a man who can't make up his mind. You get tough."

He touched her cheek. "I didn't mean to make you cry, princess. And I have made up my mind. That's why I'm here."

"And do you think I'm just going to forget what you put me through, as if it never happened?"

He glared at her, his back to the wall. "You love me. You said it in Florida, and you still do. You wouldn't have slept with me if you didn't. And I think you always will."

She shook her head. "Your humility is touching."

"Are you trying to tell me you don't?"

"Of course not. You know better. But I've been thinking lately that love isn't everything, Drew. I loved you enough for three people, and that still didn't make it work."

"That was the problem," he said, so softly that she almost didn't hear it.

"What?"

"You loved me too much."

Cindy put her hands to her temples. "Drew, you're not making sense."

"Yes, I am. Listen to me." He took her by the shoulders and looked into her eyes. "You were right when you said I was scared. In such a short time, I could see that I'd become everything to you. I didn't know if I could live up to that. You were giving me so much, all you had, and that made me want to run."

Her eyes filmed with tears. "I don't understand you. Most people are afraid they'll never be loved like that. *I'm* afraid I'll never be loved like that."

He embraced her tightly, rocking her back and forth. "You are," he murmured. "You are."

"I wish I could believe that," she sobbed.

Fox sat her in an empty chair and pulled a wad of tissues from his pocket. "I came prepared," he said, and she had to smile.

He sat on his haunches before her and took her hands. "Princess, I know I've given you a very bad time, not because I wanted to, but because I couldn't help it." He took a deep breath. "I've been alone all my life. I never trusted anyone except my family, and my job didn't exactly encourage me to believe the best about people." He brushed a loose strand of hair back from her forehead. "And then you arrived, with your satchel full of books, your gentleness, and your honor." He shrugged one shoulder slightly. "I couldn't resist you. You seemed to be everything fine and noble that was missing from my life."

"Oh, Drew," Cindy said, sniffling. "You make me sound like the Statue of Liberty or something."

"Are you going to listen?" he asked, arching an eyebrow.

"I'm listening."

"I kept telling myself," he went on, "that I would see you just one more time, and then stop, like you were a drug. But you weren't, you were something I needed in order to live, something I'd been lacking and then found."

She didn't move, her eyes fastened on his face.

"Then when you got hurt and wound up in the hospital, it looked like it was my responsibility."

"Only to you, Drew. I never thought that."

He shook his head. "Come on, Cindy, that wouldn't have happened if I were an accountant."

She was silent, unable to dispute him.

"I felt so guilty, like I had...defiled you. All I could think about was the way you looked when I brought you in to the hospital, all white and cold, as limp as a rag doll." His face changed at the memory, and she could see the impact it still had on him. "And Paula screaming at me in the emergency room, 'This is your fault! You did this to her!'"

"She was upset, Drew. She didn't know what she was saying."

"She knew," he countered quietly. "And she was right."

"I didn't blame you."

"Of course not, you wouldn't. But I blamed myself. There didn't seem to be anything to do but to let you go."

"And I had no say in the matter? That was a decision you had to make all by yourself?"

He turned her hand over in her lap and studied it. "I knew what you would say. You would have stayed with me even if you thought it would happen again. So I handled it."

"You handled it by returning my love to me like a gift you didn't wish to open."

"I'm sorry," he said, his head bent, and she believed that he was.

She touched his hair, so soft and silky, so unlike the rest of him. "Then why did you come after me, Drew? Has anything changed?"

He didn't answer for a moment, then said, "Once your thesis is accepted, and you get your degree, you'll be free to go anywhere and look for a job, right?"

"Right."

He raised his eyes to hers. "What about coming to Florida?"

"To do what?"

"Be my wife," he answered, clearly afraid that she would refuse him, but determined, as always, to complete his mission.

Cindy bent forward to rest her head on his shoulder. She put her arms around his waist and closed her eyes.

"Is that a yes?" he asked huskily, stroking her back and arms as if to assure himself of her reality.

"I want to marry you, more than anything in the world. But what you just said is still true, and I don't think I could stand worrying about you every time you went out on a case," Cindy said.

"I know. That's why I got a new job."

Cindy raised her head.

He nodded. "I'll be running a security agency in Tampa. With the connections I had from working with the police, it wasn't hard to arrange."

Cindy stared at him, hardly daring to believe it.

"I want you, princess," he said. "And I'll do anything I have to in order to get you."

"But will you be happy? Tracking has always been your life."

"I'll be happy with you. You'll be my new life."

She hugged him again, closing her eyes. "What about the differences between us?" she asked. "They seemed to bother you so much."

"We'll work them out," he said in her ear. "It's not fair to blame you and deny both of us happiness, for something my mother did over thirty years ago."

"Now why didn't I think of that?" she said, and he chuckled.

"Are you saying I should have listened to you in the first place and avoided all this conflict?" he asked her.

"Certainly not," she whispered.

"I didn't think so." He pulled back from her and stood up, looking around the room.

"Does this door lock?" he asked.

"Drew, you're not suggesting..."

"I certainly am. I've waited long enough." He picked her up and carried her to the vinyl love seat in the reading area. "This will have to do." He went to the door and locked it, then blocked it with a filing cabinet.

When he joined her, she asked, "What would you have done if Richard showed up first at the office, instead of me?"

"I'd have found you," he said grimly, unbuttoning her blouse. "I would have gotten the information out of him."

She opened her mouth to say something else, and he covered it with a large, tanned hand.

"I love you," he said, "but if you say one more word I am going to gag you."

He kissed her, and she discovered that she had nothing left to say.

Take 4
Silhouette Special Edition novels
FREE...

and preview future books in your home for 15 days!

Start with 4 FREE books, yours to keep. Then, preview 6 brand-new Special Edition® novels— delivered right to your door every month—as soon as they are published.

When you decide to keep them, pay just $1.95 each ($2.50 each in Canada), *with no shipping, handling, or other additional charges of any kind!*

Romance *is* alive, well and flourishing in the moving love stories presented by Silhouette Special Edition. They'll awaken your desires, enliven your senses, and leave you tingling all over with excitement. In each romance-filled story you'll live and breathe the emotions of love and the satisfaction of romance triumphant.

You won't want to miss a single one of the heart-felt stories presented by Silhouette Special Edition; and when you take advantage of this special offer, you won't have to.

You'll also receive a FREE subscription to the Silhouette Books Newsletter as long as you remain a member. Each lively issue is filled with news on upcoming titles, interviews with your favorite authors, even their favorite recipes.

To become a home subscriber and receive your first 4 books FREE, fill out and mail the coupon today!

Silhouette Special Edition®

Silhouette Books, 120 Brighton Rd., P.O. Box 5084, Clifton, NJ 07015-5084

Take 4 Silhouette Intimate Moments novels FREE...

If you're the kind of woman who wants more passion from your romance novels...

... preview 4 brand new Silhouette Intimate Moments® novels—delivered right to your door every month—for 15 days as soon as they are published. When you decide to keep them, you pay just $2.25 each ($2.50 each, in Canada), *with no shipping, handling, or other charges of any kind!*

These romance novels are not for everyone. They were created to give you a more detailed, more exciting reading experience, filled with romantic fantasy...dynamic, contemporary characters... involving stories...intense sensuality and stirring passion.

If that's the kind of romance reading you're looking for, Silhouette Intimate Moments novels were created for you.

The first 4 Silhouette Intimate Moments selections are absolutely FREE and without obligation, yours to keep! You can cancel at any time.

You'll also receive a FREE subscription to the Silhouette Books Newsletter as long as you remain a member. Its filled with news on upcoming books, interviews with your favorite authors, even their favorite recipes.

To get your first 4 Silhouette Intimate Moments novels FREE, fill out and mail the coupon today!

Silhouette Intimate Moments®

Silhouette Books, 120 Brighton Rd., P.O. Box 5084, Clifton, NJ 07015-5084

 **Silhouette Desire**

COMING NEXT MONTH

THE FIRE OF SPRING—Elizabeth Lowell
Winning the Sheridan ranch wasn't enough for vengeful
Logan Garrett—he wanted Dawn Sheridan, too. Dawn was
determined to teach him to love, not hate, and she'd accept
nothing less.

THE SANDCASTLE MAN—Nicole Monet
Sharon wanted a child—Michael's child, but Michael was gone.
Then one day Sharon met Rob Barnes, who became her fairy-tale
prince...but would reality intrude on their dreams?

LOGICAL CHOICE—Amanda Lee
Analytically minded Blake Hamilton was surprised when he
discovered his attraction to Diana Adams couldn't be explained
away. Diana had to show him just how illogical love could be!

CONFESS TO APOLLO—Suzanne Carey
Denying her own Greek heritage, Zoe planned to quickly leave
her childhood home after a business trip there. Then she met
Alex Kalandris—devastatingly handsome, utterly compelling
and—Greek.

SPLIT IMAGES—Naomi Horton
After TV spokeswoman Cassidy York interviewed arrogant
Logan Wilde and got blackmailed, on-air, into a date with him,
she was enraged. But meeting the man behind the image
engendered very different emotions.

UNFINISHED RHAPSODY—Gina Caimi
When concert pianist Lauren Welles returned home to her former
music teacher, Jason Caldwell, she realized she still had a lot
more to learn.... But not about music.

AVAILABLE NOW:

OUT OF THIS WORLD
Janet Joyce

DESPERADO
Doreen Owens Malek

PICTURE OF LOVE
Robin Elliott

SONGBIRD
Syrie A. Astrahan

BODY AND SOUL
Jennifer Greene

IN THE PALM OF HER HAND
Dixie Browning